ROYAL SUMMER

ROYAL SUMMER

KASS MORGAN

HARPER
An Imprint of HarperCollins*Publishers*

HarperCollins Children's Books, a division of
HarperCollins Publishers, 195 Broadway,
New York, NY 10007

HarperCollins Publishers, Macken House,
39/40 Mayor Street Upper, Dublin 1,
D01 C9W8, Ireland

Royal Summer

harpercollins.com

Library of Congress Control Number: 2023930152
ISBN 978-0-06-328750-1

Typography by Julia Tyler
26 27 28 29 30 LBC 5 4 3 2 1

FIRST EDITION

To the brilliant Viana Siniscalchi,
for everything

1

It is a truth universally acknowledged that an American girl spending the summer in the UK must be in want of romance.

Not this girl, though.

It's something I keep trying to impress on the strangers who chat me up in the airport and on the plane.

"*Ohhh,*" a woman holding a sleeping baby says to me at the terminal. "You're spending the entire summer in Edinburgh? That's amazing. You'll have so many *adventures* there." And by "adventures," it's clear she means flings.

"I'll actually be too busy with work," I reply. When her face falls, I add, "But I'm still excited!"

And I am. So excited. I've also been awake for far too long. Sleep? I don't know her. It's amazing what a little caffeine and a lot of adrenaline will do to combat jet lag.

My flight to Edinburgh from Milwaukee (by way of Chicago) is an overnight and I have the red eyes to prove it.

I power through customs and figure out the tram situation by reminding myself that I'm here to not only meet, but work for, my hero, Margaret MacIntyre.

Hey, I want to tell my fellow small talkers. *I don't need your adventure or your romance. Not when I have one of the greatest living novelists of our time.* But people don't generally appreciate this attitude. My own parents think I'm deranged. They offered to come along with me so we could do touristy things together. Thankfully I sidestepped that potential for disaster by telling them I really need to focus on work this summer.

Unfortunately, there was a mix-up when booking my flight here, which means I'm arriving with only a couple of hours to spare before I meet Margaret MacIntyre for the first time. It's fine. I'm fine. I work great under pressure. Including the pressure to get from the airport to the flat I'll be living in this summer, arranged for me by Margaret's former assistant.

It's fine. I am *fine.*

At least I am until I get on the tram and activate my new international SIM card and I see that I have three missed calls and twelve new texts. All from the same two numbers. Two numbers I should block.

My thumb hovers, ready to do just that. Instead, I send my parents a quick text telling them I've arrived and all is well. Then I slip my phone away to take in my first views of Scotland. The sky is gray, but not in a gloomy,

I-want-to-stay-inside-and-succumb-to-ennui way. Rather, it feels like I'm a heroine in a gothic novel. I imagine myself walking the moors clad in a long dress that gets swept up in the wind, while a tortured yet gorgeous man watches me with longing.

I may have been reading *Wuthering Heights* on the plane. And when I wasn't doing that, I may have been watching *Pride & Prejudice* for the five hundredth time.

We approach a station, and I double-check the emailed instructions to ensure this is where I'm supposed to get off. I somehow manage to strap on my oversized backpack and roll my gigantic suitcase off the train without beaning any of the other passengers. It's more of an accomplishment than one would think, considering my backpack is barely smaller than I am.

I follow my GPS from the York Place tram station, glancing in store windows as I trudge along. Buttery shortbread calls to me from one shop; knitted sweaters beckon from another. As tempting as it is to drop my bags and spend all the money I have yet to earn, I stay focused and finally reach a corner restaurant with rich burgundy trim and gold lettering that says The High Road Pub. I look at the address on the little white sign stuck to the stone exterior. Then I consult the instructions with the address of my flat. I imagine myself making a bed out of tables sticky from beer and check the address again.

An elderly man with twinkling eyes comes outside to

wipe down tables and rearrange salt and pepper shakers and small bottles of vinegar.

"You look lost, lass," he says.

"I feel pretty lost," I admit. "I'm supposed to be staying here this summer, but—"

"Ah, Hannah Grant, you've arrived. Shame you're seeing Edinburgh for the first time on such a dreary day." He beams at me before shouting through the open pub door, "Eileen, our new lodger is here."

A woman with short gray hair wearing an apron comes out and claps her hands together. "You must be Hannah," she says warmly.

I extend a hand to shake hers. "I am. Thanks so much for having me."

"This is my wife, Eileen," the man says in an accent so thick I find myself leaning toward him to catch every word, "and I'm William, but you can call me Bill."

Eileen leads me to the back of the bustling pub, where she pushes aside a curtain, revealing a stairway that leads to a back door and second floor.

"This is all locked up and secure, love, no minding that. This here's your key. If the pub's closed, use this back door. You can also use it if you want to avoid all those steam-boated eejits in there," she says, handing me a comically large key chain that says "There's nae place like hame." "William and I are down the hall in our own wing. You'll have a bedroom and a WC all to yourself. The view out your window is to the back alley, but if you squint, you'll see some trees in the distance. Behind that is the Palace of Holyroodhouse."

She unlocks a door and ushers me inside my home for the summer. The walls are papered with white and blue flowers. It's worn, but cheerful. My bed is a single, with a white duvet. There's a nightstand, an armoire, and a small desk. Through an open door, I can see a toilet, pedestal sink, and a shower.

"This is perfect," I say. And it truly is. Because it's not just cheerful, it's all mine.

This is so different from my house back in Wisconsin, crammed full of miscellaneous furniture and knickknacks. My parents love nothing more than souvenirs. They're singlehandedly keeping the snow globe and mug industries alive in the US. This may be sparse, but it's homey, and I like the change.

"I'll leave you to get unpacked, dear. Dinnae hesitate to call out if you need anything," Eileen says. "We're so happy to have you."

I put my backpack on the bed and catch a glimpse of the clock on the nightstand. Oh god, how could I have lost track of the time?!

"I'm supposed to be at Margaret MacIntyre's in an hour and a half," I say, unable to keep my voice from sounding frantic. "Can you tell me how to get there? How long will it take?"

Eileen gives me a reassuring pat. "It's close, no worries there. Bill's got to deliver her early dinner anyway. He'll drop you off." She closes the door behind her and I'm alone.

I'm *alone.* In another country. About to become an assistant to my hero.

I use my nervous energy to unpack my things and take a quick shower without wetting my hair.

Unfortunately, when I look in the mirror, my reflection doesn't scream "serious literary protégé." I put on the reading glasses I barely need and a cardigan to look more academic.

I'm not ashamed to say I am fully desperate for Margaret MacIntyre to like me. I've been watching and reading every interview she's ever given, trying to determine which parts of my personality to accentuate and which to hide. I've learned the hard way that my sense of humor isn't for everyone. My cousin Willa once compared me to black licorice—*A lot of people can't stand it. But the people who do love it are* obsessed.

Kind of a weird thing to say to a twelve-year-old, now that I think about it.

But Margaret writes prickly heroines that still manage to be endearing, so I'm hoping she'll see the best in me too.

I lock my door behind me, trot down the stairs, and look for Bill. I spot him in the middle of a sea of people all wearing the same jersey, all singing a song that's unintelligible to my American ears but sounds fun. I stretch my hand above me in an attempt to get his attention. Unfortunately, my five-foot-nothing frame doesn't do me any favors.

"Sorry, love," Eileen says, thrusting a heavy, foil-covered platter into my hands. "These bampots just showed up and they're thirsty. You'll have to take the bus instead. The thirty-five bus stops right out front. Maggie's house is only four stops down. Look for the green door. Trust me, you can't miss it."

"Oh, okay, that's . . ." I adjust the messenger bag I bought specifically for this job so I can carry what I assume is Margaret MacIntyre's early dinner. I go over the directions Eileen has just given me again. "Four stops on the bus and the—"

"Aye, the green door," she says, ushering me through the pub, which is getting busier by the minute.

As I wait for the bus, praying I don't mess up and get myself fired, I calm myself by thinking back to when I first fell in love with Margaret's writing.

I was thirteen and had read pretty much everything in the school library's fiction section. While sitting at a table, reading *The Hunger Games* for the tenth time, my favorite librarian handed me a slip of paper with a list of titles written on it.

I think you're ready to meet Margaret MacIntyre, she said with a smile. *You'll have to ask your parents to buy her books or pick them up at the public library since we only stock middle grade and YA here, but she's my favorite author. She changed my life. Something tells me she'll change yours.*

The librarian was right—Margaret MacIntyre's books cast a spell over me.

It isn't just that her prose is poetic yet accessible. It isn't that her characters are so fleshed out, you forget they're fictional. It's that reading her books makes you feel seen, from the surface to the depth of your soul—the parts you're afraid to show people, the parts you're afraid make you unlovable.

I started writing fiction the day I finished my first MacIntyre book. A few years later, I read an interview where she said, "I knew I was a writer the day a writer I revered told me I was one."

From then on, I had very specific goals:

1. To meet Margaret MacIntyre
2. To hear her say, "You're a writer."
3. To get my degree in Creative Writing
4. To publish a novel
5. To keep publishing novels until I die

The bus pulls up and I get on, then freeze when I realize I left my cash in my backpack back at the pub. I'm not sure if Apple Pay works here, and I can't google to check since my hands are wrapped around the food I'm delivering. I lurch to the side and barely manage to keep my balance. "I'm sorry, I . . . I'll just." Just what? Offer the driver Margaret's dinner?

"American," the driver mutters under his breath. "Where are ya heading?"

"Um, four stops? I don't know the street name." That's when I spot the contactless payment reader. I can use my phone. Theoretically. But there's no way for me to pull it out of my back pocket while holding the platter, and I can't risk spilling that all over the bus. Clenching my teeth with embarrassment, I tilt my hip toward the reader and pray that it'll scan through my jeans.

It doesn't, of course. I try again, this time making full contact with the scanner.

The bus driver shakes his head and sighs. "Just take a seat." The subtext is clear: Please stop rubbing your butt against the equipment.

I thank him profusely and, face burning, take a seat close to the front so I don't have to look at the other passengers who just watched a weird American girl try to twerk against the card reader. *Just four stops*, I tell myself, eyes fixed on the screen that lists the stop names. After the third stop, I balance the tray in my lap, press the red button on the pole next to me, and when the bus pulls up to the curb, do my best to exit in a dignified manner.

Once I'm on the sidewalk, I take a deep breath. Okay, time for a fresh start. Everything is going to be fine. I make my way down a quiet street lined with buildings made of sandstone and limestone, in search of a green door. It takes me no time to find it and I immediately understand why Eileen said I can't miss it. The buildings, all connected, have the same white-ish rectangular front doors with the same semicircle window overtop. All, except for one.

Just when I thought I couldn't admire her more, Margaret MacIntyre's house features a gothic door the color of jade. Even better? There are adorable Highland cow faces made of brass and the knockers are brass rings through the cows' noses. Balancing the tray with one hand, I knock, hoping whatever I'm carrying is still cold or hot or whatever it's supposed to be.

The door swings open and I am face-to-face with the person who changed my life.

"Margaret MacIntyre," I say, in complete shock. The tray slips from my hands and lands on her front step with a clatter. My now-empty hands fly to my mouth.

But Margaret MacIntyre opens her arms and says, "You must be my assistant all the way from America."

I open my arms too and I am *hugging one of the greatest modern novelists of my time.* Of *all* time.

"I'm so sorry about your dinner," I tell her, my cheek tickled by her wiry black hair. I stoop to pick up the tray.

"Now my potatoes are mashed *and* smashed," she says

with a laugh that could light up the dreary sky. She pulls back and takes a look at me. "Well, Hannah Grant, I hope you're ready to work."

"I'm ready," I promise, already certain this is going to be the greatest summer of my entire life.

2

I spend two glorious hours in Margaret's company. She shares her dinner of hearty steak-and-ale pie and a side of mashed (now smashed) potatoes with me, and we talk about books and music and travel and life.

My main job as her assistant this summer is as simple as it is real: to make sure she writes. If I see her spending too much time scrolling through Instagram Reels, I'm supposed to bring her a cup of tea and some candy and take her phone away. I literally cannot imagine doing such a thing, but she made me swear on a copy of *Anne of Green Gables* that I would. Her new book jumps around in time, which means my other responsibilities will be continuity and research, so she isn't slowed down by details. I'm so excited I can hardly breathe.

"This has been a delight," Margaret tells me as she walks me to the door. "Tomorrow, we work."

"I can't wait," I tell her, beaming.

Penniless and poundless without my wallet—and uncertain whether my Apple Pay works internationally—I decide to walk rather than risk another bus ride. I'm on such a high, I'm certain I could float back to the pub.

It's so strange, feeling this way and having no one to talk to about my day. The streets of Edinburgh are alive with commuters staring at their phones, trying to make it to their next destinations: groups of friends holding on to one another and laughing, families going to dinner. A pang of loneliness hits me as I weave between them all. I pull out my own phone, expecting to see more missed calls, more messages. When nothing new is there, I can't decide whether I'm relieved or depressed. I roll my shoulders back and resolve not to let anything I've left behind in Milwaukee ruin what has been an imperfectly perfect day in Scotland.

I don't need any of them. This summer is about me, I tell myself as I reach the corner where the sign for The High Road becomes visible. I'm so eager to tell someone about my magical afternoon with Margaret, I'm sort of hoping Bill or Eileen will have time to chat with me.

The High Road in the evening is a completely different vibe from the afternoon. Eileen and Bill are nowhere to be seen, replaced instead with younger staff, and the crowd is decidedly less *Let's put on a Tom Jones record* and more *Have you heard the latest Chappell Roan?*

One group in particular catches my attention. There's a

muscular, attractive Black man confidently wearing a tank top that says "I'm cool, but I cry a lot," and a white girl with long dark hair that looks magenta when the light hits it, who's laughing uproariously. She's clutching the arm of a tall guy with copper hair and a bemused smile. I'm mesmerized by their energy and don't even realize I'm standing in the way of anyone until I feel a bump behind me and something wet sloshes onto my back.

"Ohmygod, I'm so sorry," a horrified English voice says.

I turn around and see a South Asian girl, who looks about my age and is so gorgeous she deserves her own Sephora line.

"No, it's my fault," I insist. "I was standing here like an eejit, I mean *idiot*." The word slipped out before I realized what I was saying. *You've been here less than twenty-four hours*, I remind myself. *You do* not *get to use Scottish slang*.

The girl's face turns from apologetic to delighted in an instant. "I found an American," she yells to the group I was staring at.

"Why'd you pour your drink on her, then?" the muscular guy asks. He waves me over. "Come here so we can apologize on Bethany's behalf and pick your brain."

"Please come talk to us," the girl I've just learned is named Bethany says. "Callum is obsessed with America, and I owe you a pint as an apology."

I wonder if Callum is the muscular guy or the copper-haired guy with the smirk. Before I know it, I'm seated at a table with a beer in front of me while Bethany is retreating to the bar to get another one. The other three approach the table, looking at me expectantly. I feel like I'm in a zoo.

"Hi," I say with an awkward wave.

"She's adorable," the girl with the magenta hair coos.

"She's better than adorable," the copper-haired guy says. "She looks like she could've been a pinup girl in the nineteen fifties."

"Not tonight," Magenta-Hair says, hitting him in the arm. "Take one night off, I beg of you."

Oh, he is trouble.

"I just want to hear her talk all night so I can appreciate her accent," the muscular guy says. "I want to know how many times she's been to Universal Studios and if she's ever seen the Grand Canyon."

The copper-haired smooth talker takes the seat beside me. His jawline is ridiculous.

"Stop talking about her like she's not here," he says. I've never been quite sure what "plummy" means, but I'm pretty sure it applies to his English accent. In fact, none of them sound Scottish. At least, not to my untrained ear.

"Yeah," I agree, turning to him. "Stop talking about 'her' like she's not here."

The other two laugh and I'm not sure why it's quite so funny that I called him out on his hypocrisy. Meanwhile, the girl who bumped into me, Bethany, returns and sits on the other side of me. "Have you lot been raised in a barn? Introduce yourselves!"

"I'm Callum." The guy in the tank top reaches his hand out to shake mine. He nudges the girl with magenta hair. "That's Mhairi. The girl who spilled on you is Bethany."

"I'm Hannah," I say. There's a pause. I jut a thumb at the guy beside me. "Does he not have a name or is he just not worth knowing?"

The shriek of laughter that comes from the other three is contagious, but I manage to keep a straight face, mostly because I have no idea what's so funny. I take a sip of beer. It's quite hoppy and I'm not normally a beer drinker, but I *am* legal here. When in Scotland, et cetera.

I turn to the nameless guy. "And you are . . . ?"

"Finn," he says, scrutinizing me so intensely, I wonder if I have something on my face. I lick my lips in case there's foam on them and catch his eye for just a millisecond. He flashes me a knowing look and raises one eyebrow.

I have half a mind to scooch my chair farther away from him and half a mind to scooch it closer.

"What are you doing in Edinburgh?" Mhairi asks. She's fidgety and energetic. She hasn't stopped playing with the container of sugar packets since we all sat down.

"I have a job here. I just arrived today."

"No wonder you looked so lost, standing there in the middle of the pub," Bethany says sympathetically.

"Yes, aren't you lucky Bethany spilled on you," Finn says to me. "Or are *we* the lucky ones?"

I roll my eyes as if I'm irritated by the cheesy innuendo. But the truth is, my heart is racing.

"Finally, someone immune to your charms," Mhairi practically sings.

Despite the player energy from Finn, I do feel lucky to be brought into a group of people right when I was feeling alone.

"I'm here for the summer," I explain to the rest of the group, deliberately ignoring Finn. The only way to deal with a player is to ignore him.

"Don't you love the way she says 'summer'?" Callum asks Mhairi, hitting the hard *r* sound. "If she says 'y'all' next, I'll *die*."

"Not likely," I say with a laugh. "I'm from Milwaukee, not the south. And I thought being American was out of fashion these days."

"Darling, no." Callum shakes his head emphatically. "America has got a lot of things wrong, but do you know what it's gotten right?" He starts counting off on his fingers. "Pop girlies, enormous shopping malls, Disney Gays—"

"Gas-guzzling SUVs," Finn says dryly. "Manipulative pharmaceutical ads on television. Confusing cash notes that are all the same color. Jake Paul."

Is he *negging* me? Like some wannabe pickup artist?

Callum glares at Finn, then continues. "Ensemble sitcoms that run for more than two years, podcasts about reality shows about reality stars who have been in more than one reality show—"

"Someone, *please* shut him up," Bethany cries dramatically.

Mhairi begins throwing sugar packets at Callum, and he catches every single one while saying, "Hannah, if I give you money, can you get me kitschy American souvenirs I can decorate my house with?"

"My own house is full of them," I tell him. "I'll just send you the ones my parents collect."

Callum gasps so dramatically, the entire table laughs.

Finn leans in so close, his breath moves my hair. "Now look what you've done."

I turn my head and try to ignore the swoop my stomach does when I stare into his hazel eyes. "I find *him* delightful. You, on the other hand . . ."

He sits up and looks at me expectantly. "I'm what? Go on, you can say it."

"You're a rapscallion," I tell him, and take a sip of beer.

"A *rapscallion*?" Finn gives me a wry smile. "Does every American girl talk like my nan?"

I blame the word choice on the series of historical romances I read to get through senior year.

"Definitely. Nan-core is the new thing," I say blithely. "I bet she'd be really popular in America."

The table is now staring at us. Shit, did I say something wrong? Maybe Finn's grandma just died or something. To break the awkwardness, I ask, "How do you all know each other? From school? You're not Scottish, right?"

Mhairi snort-laughs into her pint.

"Yeah," Bethany says, exchanging looks with the others. "We go to uni together, but . . ."

"But what?" I can't shake the feeling that I'm missing something. An inside joke or a secret. It's starting to make me self-conscious.

"But that's it," Finn says, cutting her off. "It's summer holiday, and those three rented a flat in Edinburgh for fun. They let me crash there when I get too sloshed."

It sounds reasonable, but the cagey way he says it makes me think it's not entirely true.

"The real reason the three of us got a flat here for the summer," Bethany says meaningfully, "is because our main job is to keep *that one*"—she nods at Finn—"out of trouble."

"There's no trouble here," Finn says, stretching his arms out and casually resting one on the back of my chair.

"Oh please," I say, lifting his arm off and giving it back to him. "Does this act ever really work for you?"

There's that look again between them.

"This has literally never happened before," Bethany says to Callum and Mhairi.

"Is it possible that Americans are immune to Finn?" Callum asks.

"We know *that* isn't true. But maybe it's a Midwestern thing," Mhairi says thoughtfully.

I am absolutely missing something crucial. Or jet lag is finally taking its toll. A song comes on and Callum, Mhairi, and Bethany all suddenly squeal.

"I *need* to dance," Callum insists.

Maybe the only thing I'm missing is that Finn really is a rapscallion. A rogue. A rake. Some other term from this century that means he leaves messes for his friends to clean up. Well, I've sworn off relationships so no danger here.

Of course, that doesn't mean I might not try to torture him a little. For my own amusement.

"Go dance," I tell them. "I'll make sure your friend doesn't get into trouble."

They don't hesitate to run away, despite the clear lack of a dance floor. They find an area big enough to do some choreographed moves that are surprisingly good. Instead of getting annoyed, other patrons slowly join in on the fun.

"Don't think I don't know what you're doing," Finn says. There's a hint of irritation that makes me want to laugh. "Plenty of girls have tried this angle. It never works."

"*What* angle?" I'm growing a bit tired of all these cagey comments, and can't keep a note of exasperation out of my voice.

He stares at me for a long moment, then his face softens

into the first genuine smile I've seen from him. A strange feeling of warmth spreads through my chest while warning bells ring in my head. The last thing I need this summer is a distraction, no matter how handsome he is. I have a tendency to catch feelings when I shouldn't. This is the worst type of guy to catch feelings for. It's time to change the subject. "So you're not a dancer?" I say, nodding at his friends.

"I'm supposed to stick to the Viennese waltz," he says dryly. "Family policy, you know."

"Your family has a policy on dancing? Are you some weird cult?"

"In a sense. So tell me, American Hannah. What brings you to a country you know nothing about?"

"Who says I know nothing about Scotland?" Truth be told, I don't, beyond Margaret MacIntyre, *Outlander*, *Macbeth*, a little Robbie Burns, and whatever I read in my travel book.

"Call it a hunch. I'm genuinely curious why you're here."

I consider my answer while I look over the crowd. There's a high-top populated with men in suits who are giving a group of women the once-over. Some elderly men, all sporting white beards and flat caps, are laughing uproariously at a story one of them is telling. Meanwhile, Finn's friends are now doing a dance I vaguely recognize from TikTok.

I may not be Scottish, and I may have the beginning

tugs of homesickness—despite everything I want to leave behind—but I don't feel out of place here, which is why I settle on the undressed truth.

"I'm here because I need the author I admire most in the world to read my work and tell me I'm a writer so that I can go to college in the fall, become an English major, and pursue the rest of the life I've already got planned out."

"And that author lives in Edinburgh," Finn says. I nod. "What happens if the writer is an absolute knob—"

"She's not."

"What happens if the non-knob writer doesn't comply? Then the rest of your life . . . ?"

I'd never even considered it not happening as a possibility. In my experience, you make a plan, and then you execute that plan. I meet his gaze and hold it. My control of my tongue slips and the words fall out of me. "I don't know what happens. But I'm scared to find out."

Finn looks thoughtful. He puts his palms out. "Give me your hands."

"Why?" I ask, guarded.

"Are all Americans so difficult? Come on, Marilyn Monroe. Hands," he commands, shaking his head. The waves of his copper hair shake back and forth. I swear they're calling me a chicken.

I put my hands in his and try not to shiver from their

warmth. To hide my reaction, I quip, "Your hands are really soft. Do you get regular manicures?"

"Of course I do." Instead of pulling away, he holds my hands a little firmer, though not unpleasantly so, and examines my nails. They're currently painted red with white polka dots. "Though clearly I need to change manicurists because whoever's doing yours is putting mine to shame."

"I paint them myself," I tell him, mostly because I'm afraid if I change the subject, he'll let go of me. Perhaps he is in fact a rapscallion, but he's also magnetic. *Who is this guy? What's his story?* He gives my hands a little shake.

"Hannah. Pay attention. This is important."

I laugh. "All right, Finn. Change my life."

"You are already a writer," he tells me gravely.

Whatever I could have imagined him saying, I never would've come up with that. I roll my eyes and pull my hands away. "Sorry, it doesn't work that way. It can't just be some random British guy in a pub who tells me that. It has to be someone with authority."

"Maybe I'm not 'random.' Maybe I do have authority. Or maybe this is all nonsense and the only person who needs to tell you you're a writer is you."

Finn's friends return in a flurry of hand gestures and shaking of phones and words I can't quite make out.

"Just calm down," Finn tells them, but he looks rattled.

"What's going on?" I ask. Did an angry ex-girlfriend

storm in? Or does he owe someone money? Finn gives off rich-kid vibes, but you never know.

"We have *to go now,*" Bethany insists. "We've been spotted."

"We have to leave, like, five minutes ago," Mhairi adds.

I look at their concerned faces. "Are you all fugitives? Are the cops after you?"

No one's paying attention to me and they're all talking on top of each other. I hear Bethany say something about a backdoor exit, to which Callum makes a joke that gets a snort out of both Finn and Mhairi.

"If you're looking for a way out, I know one," I tell them. "I actually live here. Upstairs, I mean. I can show you the door I use." They all start thanking me at the same time, but I cut them off. "But only if you promise me I'm not going to be, like, questioned by the police later or something." I can see the headline now: "Jet-Lagged American Helps Wanted Criminals Escape from Pub."

The chattering stops as they appear to have a silent conversation.

"I still follow my toxic ex on Snapchat," Callum finally says to me, pocketing his phone. "The little map says he's headed this way, and I simply cannot."

"No problem." I stand up, well-versed on the topic of toxic exes. "Follow me."

I lead them toward the back hallway and point out the door Eileen told me to use when the pub's closed.

Callum, Mhairi, and Bethany each give me a hug as they exit one by one. Finn stops in front of me. I wonder if he's going to give me a hug too. For a split second, I wonder if he's going to live up to his reputation and try and kiss me. He doesn't.

"You're a lifesaver," he says. "The best thing to come out of America since the cheesesteak sandwich."

"And you're the one girls are supposed to find irresistible?"

He looks as though he's about to say something else, then shakes his head.

"See you around, rapscallion," I call after him and close the door before he can reply. It's a throwaway line because I never expect to see that guy again. And I'm certain that's for the best.

3

Not being a morning person, I've never actually leaped out of bed before. I certainly didn't expect to do so when I'm fighting the effects of jet lag. But I'm on a high from my adventures yesterday—bonding with my favorite author, flirting with a boy, albeit one I'll never seen again—and can't wait to see what today holds.

I shower, fight my hair that really wants to give in to the natural humidity here, and end up sticking it on top of my head in a messy bun. At the very least, it gives a few more inches to my less-than-impressive height.

Once I'm dressed, I head to the private little kitchen where Eileen and Bill are having tea and toast.

"There's the lass," Bill says. "How are you faring so far?"

"Pretty well, I think," I say as Eileen sets a plate of toast and preserves in front of me. I tell them about meeting Margaret for the first time and the responsibilities I'll have this summer. The scene is so domestic, I feel a pang of guilt that I haven't called my parents yet. I'm just not sure what sort of mood I'll find them in, and I'm not ready to get sucked back into their drama.

My parents got pregnant with me on their second date and decided to "do the right thing" and get married before I was born. They also got married before realizing that they don't like each other very much. My mom vents to me about my dad, my dad vents to me about my mom, and any time I suggest they take some time apart, they look aghast and say, *You want to break up our* family*?*

When I got the chance to spend the summer in Edinburgh, I didn't even hesitate.

I arrive at Margaret's door ten minutes early and debate sitting on a nearby bench versus knocking on those adorable brass Highland cows. Deciding that being early shows initiative, I take ahold of the ring through one of the cow's noses and knock. There's scuttling behind the door and I hear her voice holler, "Just give me a wee second," followed by more scuttling. Eventually, the door swings open.

The Margaret I met yesterday was put together. The Margaret before me now is scattered, at best. Her black hair is sticking out at all ends; her cheeks are flushed; the buttons on her blouse aren't through the correct loops. Seeing her this way feels wrong, like spying or something, so I look down. She has only one sock on.

Either she slept late and was rushing this morning or

I've committed "coitus interruptus," and she has a partner waiting for her in the bedroom.

Please don't let it be the second scenario, I swear to myself. *I am not emotionally prepared for that kind of awkwardness with my new boss.* I vow to never be early to anything again. Ever.

I'm about to apologize when Margaret says with a happy sigh, "Oh, my dear, the most wonderful thing has happened this morning."

I pray she isn't about to tell me the story of how she got laid. I'm progressive—I hope Margaret is getting hers if that's what she wants—but I am also a repressed Midwesterner.

"Come in, come in," Margaret says, shutting the door behind me. "We've got to have a wee talk, you and I, and I truly hope, dear, that you won't hate me by the end of it."

"I could never hate you," I tell her, because I couldn't. She's created characters that will be my lifelong friends. She's invented worlds I've escaped to when my own life has been frustrating or scary or even just boring. Despite all that, there's a pit in my stomach, an instinct kicking into high gear. Something's off and it isn't just her appearance.

We go to her study, a room I'd happily move into. There's a gorgeous antique desk covered in papers, various pens and sticky notes in myriad colors, and an open laptop. Every wall is a bookshelf. She even has one of those sliding ladders. Talk about living the dream.

Margaret sits in one of two plush, mustard-yellow chairs tucked in the corner of the room and gestures that I should take the other one, a delicate table between us.

"Before we start," she says, "can I get you any tea?"

"I'm fine, thanks," I tell her. I tried drinking tea at breakfast this morning with Bill and Eileen, and I do *not* get the appeal. But really, I don't want to delay the news any further.

What could she say that would make me hate her? Has she decided to change directions with her book, and I suddenly need to become an expert in the Byzantine era to help her? Or maybe she wants me to use a Scottish accent while I'm here because she finds my American pronunciations gauche, she—

"I'm seeing someone," she says. Her eyes sparkle as she brings her hands together in a prayer position under her chin.

"Oh." *Oh.* I relax. Margaret MacIntyre wants to have girl talk with me. I can do girl talk. "That's so exciting!"

"In my next book, I was planning on writing about a woman who rediscovers herself while in a relationship with a younger man, but I never thought it would happen to me." She leans in conspiratorially. "He's only *forty-three.*"

Huh. Margaret must be older than I realized. "What's he like?" I ask.

She leans back until her head is resting on the chair. "How do you describe a person who feels new and old to you at the same time? He's clever, he's kind. He has the greatest heart of anyone I've ever met."

"I'm so happy for you," I tell her, and I mean it. Even though hearing someone else talk about a happy relationship causes my insides to feel pinched. "Will I get to meet him?"

The sparkle drains from her face, and she sits up. "That's the thing, Hannah. He was just here on holiday. He lives in Japan, and this morning he asked me to move there with him."

I stare at her, uncomprehending.

"I decided immediately that I'm going. What have I got to lose? I mean, look at me." She gestures to herself. "I'm at a time in my life where I have to doff the expectations I've set for myself."

"Wow," I say, struggling to catch up. I can't imagine moving anywhere for a guy, and here Margaret's doing it at her age. "Are you leaving after the summer, or . . ."

She reaches across to touch the arm of my chair, her eyes growing sorrowful. "I'm sorry. I . . . We have an expression in Scotland: 'Be happy you're living, you're a long time dead.' I have to do this, Hannah. And I am so very sorry that you're the collateral damage in this decision."

"What about your book?" I ask faintly.

"I've learned long ago that I don't have to chase the muses—those lasses chase me," she says with a wink.

There's still an ember of hope in my stomach. She may

still want me to stay and work. I may still have this summer abroad I desperately need.

Margaret pats the arm of the chair and stands up. "I'm so sorry, I know this throws quite the wrench in your plans, and you must think I'm a right fool for running after a man like this."

I do think she's a fool. I don't say so. Every female character Margaret MacIntyre has ever written has chosen herself over a man. I can't believe she's doing this.

"So this job, working for you, it's . . . it's . . . done?" I'm undercaffeinated and overwhelmed and nothing is making sense. I stand up too, understanding only that our conversation is coming to a close.

She pulls me in for a hug. "I feel terrible for disappointing you this way. I'll pay for your flight home, of course."

The ember is officially extinguished, making room for panic. I grip the fabric of my shirt and try to swallow. "I can't go home. I can't go back there. Not this summer. I can't do it."

Margaret looks at me with compassion. "Again, I am so sorry. Ah, but Hannah. I promise you can figure it all out. You're young, you're smart. The world is at your feet."

It literally never feels that way, Mags, I want to tell her.

"If you change your mind," she continues, her face still full of apology, "and need the money for the flight home, you can let me know."

My head is swimming with confusion and anger as she leads me out of her house and wishes me well.

Despite the numbness taking over, my feet manage to move one in front of the other as I make my way off her street. I don't know where I'm headed but eventually I find myself at the Royal Mile. If I weren't feeling so hopeless, I could appreciate the fact that Edinburgh Castle is in the distance, the first castle I've ever seen in real life. I'd planned to come to the Royal Mile on my first day off to appreciate the history, the Scottish baronial architecture. Do some shopping. But I can barely see it through the glassy lens of my tears.

I'm out of a job, which means I'm also homeless. The flat at Bill and Eileen's was arranged and going to be paid for through Margaret.

I'm thousands of miles away from everyone I know.

As dire as that fact is, it's not even the worst part. The worst part is I never got to share my writing with Margaret MacIntyre. I never got to hear her tell me I'm a writer.

I start walking faster and farther, pushing through the crowds of the Royal Mile until my feet hurt and the tears I've been holding back stream down my cheeks. Every plan I had for myself just shattered because Margaret MacIntyre got herself a boyfriend. This is total and utter garbage.

I swipe at my tears, fatigue taking over as subtly as a cannon. I slump down until I'm sitting on the curb in front of a row of multicolored shops, all bright blues and pinks and whites. Tourists and locals alike grumble as they step around me, but I don't care.

This was supposed to be my summer of escape. My summer of grand plans and ambition. Within twenty-four hours of being here, it transformed into a summer of complete and total horseshit.

Men ruin everything.

4

Glumly, I head in the direction I'm assuming the pub is in, trying to force myself to accept this new reality: to call Margaret and take her up on the offer to buy me a ticket home. I can't. When I try to picture myself getting on that plane and returning to Milwaukee, my mind goes blank. It will not compute. It *refuses* to compute.

I take several wrong turns, a stupid little salmon swimming upstream during rush hour, and somehow end up home. Or rather, what was supposed to be my home for the summer. When I go to put the key in the door and let myself in the back entrance, I freeze. What am I going to do up there in my quaint little flat? Start packing? Draft an email to Margaret asking for the flight money? Call my parents?

I put the keys back in my bag, let it drop onto the ground, and lean my back against the brick wall. Feeling something sturdy behind me is a small comfort.

"Let me guess," a voice says. "You're upset because you

met the love of your life last night and you're afraid you'll never see him again."

Even though we'd spent less than an hour together, I immediately recognize the upper-class British accent. Still, my eyes widen at seeing Finn. Not only did I assume I'd never see this guy again, but he's catching me at my worst (I'm not one of those pretty criers).

I sniff and try to play it cool. "Oh great. Not only am I unemployed and homeless, I've got a stalker."

Finn leans against the wall. "What do you mean, you're unemployed and homeless? What's changed so quickly?"

"The author I was working for ran off to chase a man. The job was the reason I had a place to stay." I let out a quivery sigh. "I think I have to fly back to the States as soon as I can get a flight."

Something flickers in his face. "What if you got a job today?"

I'd laugh if I weren't so miserable. "That's a long shot."

"Not if I help you."

I cock my head. "Are you offering to help me pass out résumés? Or do *you* want to hire me to help you find strategic exits in pubs?"

"Neither."

I'm losing patience with what I'm sure most people regard as charm.

"I don't have time for this. I've got to go pack." I pick up my bag and get my keys out.

"*Wait*," he says. "I have a . . . *contact* at Inveresk. The castle there, rather. The royal family's Scottish residence."

"You've got a contact with the royal family," I say skeptically.

"I said I have a contact there. Someone who can get you a job."

"You're suggesting I work at a *castle*? What would I do there? Be a beefeater?"

"Those are at the Tower of London. Though you would look quite fetching in one of those fur hats."

"So what's the job, then?"

"Are you saying you want to know more about . . . the position?"

He gives me a sultry stare at the word "position," and I jangle my keys, threatening to leave again.

"I was referring to the job position. Not what we could do with our leisure time. You'll need to get your mind out of the gutter if you want to work at a castle."

I put my key in the door and begin to turn the knob. My threat doesn't make him rush. In fact, he seems to really be dragging this out.

"I'm thinking along the lines of, say . . . working in the gift shop?"

Working at a gift shop. In a castle. It's hard for me to wrap my head around the prospect, so I stall for time. "What were you doing here this afternoon anyway? Were you looking for me?"

A slightly embarrassed smile takes over his admittedly handsome face. "Just trying to walk off my hangover."

I narrow my eyes. "Why are you being so nice? Is it because I didn't sleep with you and that's made me infinitely more interesting?"

"What are you like?" He shakes his head. "Here I am, coming to apologize for our behavior last night, and you keep bringing the conversation around to sex." He pauses thoughtfully. "Though, in fairness, it *is* entirely possible I find you interesting because you've been playing hard to get."

In the back of my mind I'm warming to the idea of working at a castle. But I want to make some things very clear with Finn before I tell *him* that.

"What if I tell you there's zero chance of me ever hooking up with you? Do I still get the job?"

"You drive a hard bargain," he says with a grin. "But yes, you'll be safe from me. Only tourists go to Inveresk Castle."

I pretend to continue to deliberate even though the voice in my head is yelling at me: *Inveresk Castle or go home to my parents and Gigi and Dean? How is this even a question?*

"Okay," I say, when I feel enough time has passed. "I'd love that job, if it's available."

His hazel eyes light up. "All right, American Hannah. Now, what about that homeless problem? Do you need me to sort that too?"

I look back at the pub. "I'll have to ask Bill and Eileen how much they charge and see if I can afford rent. Could I commute to Inveresk every day?"

"No worries," he says, practically cutting me off. "I'll get you accommodations at the castle grounds, so you don't have to worry about how expensive Edinburgh is or how maddening it is to commute."

"You're going to get me a place to stay too," I say slowly, not as a question so much as a fact I'm trying to work through. This is starting to fall under the category of "too good to be true." "If this is a long con to murder me, it's really convoluted."

"Fair point. I suppose I'll have to skip the whole murder and just get you the job and the room."

I want to laugh but refuse to give him the satisfaction. I'm still not convinced this isn't a long con to get into my pants. Or *trousers*, I should say.

"Shall you give me your number so I can report back?"

I nod and take his outstretched phone, typing in my number. Warning bells are ringing in my ears as our hands linger a little too long during the exchange.

"I best be off, then," he says and gives me a rakish wink. "I've got a helpless American to save."

"I'm not helpless," I holler to him as he walks away.

"You were before I got here," he tosses over his shoulder.

I open the back door and trot up the stairs. In the safe refuge of my room, I replay the day over and over again in my mind, from my talk with Margaret to accepting Finn's help. Desperate to get someone else's opinion, I pick up my phone and am about to click on Gigi's number. It's muscle memory. Thankfully, I hang up before it starts to ring.

Calling my parents is tempting. Things are likely awkward between them without me there as a buffer. I'm certain they'll try to convince me to just come home and work at the smoothie shop at the mall since my mom's friends with the owner. I flop onto the bed and close my eyes. I may not know what I want right now, I just know I don't want that.

In the distance, I can hear muffled voices coming from the direction of Bill and Eileen's kitchen. They've been so welcoming, they might be open to batting around this idea with me. Besides, they'll know a lot more about Inveresk Castle than I do.

When I reach the kitchen, I see I've caught them on a break. They're seated at the small table, each with a cup of tea and a sandwich in front of them.

"Ah, there's the lass," Bill says upon seeing me.

"Shouldn't you be at Maggie's?" Eileen asks.

I'm about to tell them she's running off with a boyfriend and check myself. I may be upset, but I'm not unprofessional and petty. Instead, I say, "Plans have changed and she's leaving the country. Which means, I'm out of a job."

Bill and Eileen exchange a concerned look, and then Bill

gets up to pour me a cup of tea while Eileen pulls out a chair, encouraging me to sit.

"We have our summer hires filled here already, love," Eileen says apologetically. "I'm afraid we don't have the shifts to offer you at the pub."

"Oh, no, no." I wave off her thoughtfulness and accompanying dismay. "This obviously isn't your problem to solve. But I know Margaret's team had arranged for me to stay here and—"

"Never ye mind. You stay here for a few days and get your legs underneath you." Bill places a steaming cup of tea in front of me.

I choke down a sip because they're being so kind. "Something has come up—an opportunity—and I wanted to get your take on it, if that's okay?" They nod for me to continue. "I might be able to get a job at Inveresk Castle. In the gift shop."

"Oh, lovely," Eileen says. "We haven't been to Inveresk in, what, ten years, Bill? It was when your cousin was visiting from Australia."

"No, no, that was when we went to the whiskey tasting and ya got—"

"Don't you say it. I haven't been pie-eyed since before we were married. I told you, I was coming down with the flu."

Eileen tuts at him, and they return their focus to me.

"Inveresk Castle is a fine place to work for the summer," Bill says.

"Oh, it's better than fine: It's a lovely spot with the grounds and the history," Eileen adds. "But a bit far to commute by bus every day."

I explain that I'm fairly sure I have a place to stay there but would appreciate keeping my room here until everything is organized. "I can pay you, obviously," I add, unsure how much that will set me back and already wary of calling my parents to ask them for money—especially knowing they'll try to talk me into coming back.

Eileen gives me a wink. "Oh, no you won't. We'll be charging Maggie. Imagine her running off last minute like that, leaving you in a lurch."

I thank them both and nearly hug them. The grandparent vibes they give off are strong and make me feel like I've known them forever. Then I go to my room to read and wait to hear back from Finn.

Putting my future in the hands of this rapscallion seems like a very bad idea, indeed. But what other choice do I have? This was the summer that was going to change my life, and I refuse to give up.

I can't go back to being the girl I used to be.

5

American Hannah, I'm officially your hero. I made some calls, pleaded with the embassy, broke into Buckingham Palace to bargain with the king and queen, and have secured you a position at Inveresk Castle's gift shop. You will also have a place to stay there. Not all heroes wear capes, as they say, though they do all seem to be as handsome as I am.

—Finn

You've put me in a precarious position, Finn (do NOT say "that's what she said"). I want to thank you profusely, but you seem to have patted yourself on the back enough for both of us. If I compliment you at all, I fear your ego will become so inflated, you'll simply float away, your life becoming a modern-day Around the World in Eighty Days.

. . . But, thank you. You saved me from a difficult summer back home. I appreciate it.

—American Hannah (I assume there are at least a handful of your conquests in your phone who share my name and that's why you've given me a descriptor)

PS What time should I be there?

"He's been in one of his moods." My mom's lowering her voice even though I'm sure she's said these exact words to my dad at least three times today. "He isn't sleeping at night because of his back, and instead of doing something about it, he bites everyone's head off who tries to help. I just offered to get him an ibuprofen and he—"

"Would you like to hear about my trip so far?" I ask, trying to keep my patience in check. I glance at the clock. It's still too early to leave for Inveresk.

"Of course!" Mom says. "I'm dying to know—"

"Is that Tinkerbell?" I hear Dad cut her off. "Hand me the phone."

"Wait your turn," Mom says.

"I have to head out in five, so it makes sense for me to talk first."

"We've *talked* about this," Mom snaps, then turns her attention back to me. "Sorry. What were you saying?"

I suppress a sigh. There's no way I can recount all my

misadventures like this. I learned long ago that there's no use in trying to have a real conversation when my parents are in the same room. "Nothing to report."

"Really? Tell me about the—hold on, your father is insisting he go first." Before I can object, I hear rustling and then my dad's voice. "Hey, kid," he says.

"Hi, Dad," I say, forcing cheerfulness.

"Gigi stopped by. She says she hasn't heard from you and—"

"Okay, I'll reach out," I lie. "I gotta go, Dad. I've got to get to work."

"Good luck with that Maggie MacWhatever Her Name Is," he says jovially.

My mom tries to take the phone back. I know she'll want to complain about my dad some more, so I swiftly say my good-byes and hang up. Before I put my phone away, I read the final texts of the exchange I had with Finn last night one more time:

> You can report to Inveresk at noon. I'll meet you there and help get you sorted.

> Please don't embarrass my country or yours.

I'd responded:

> I'm guessing the only embarrassing thing I could do in either country is admitting to knowing you.

When he didn't reply after that, I became nervous that I took the teasing too far and offended him, so I followed it up with a more sincere message.

> Hey, British Finn: Thanks again for helping me. I don't know how or why you did it, but I do appreciate it. We have a beautiful expression back in the good ol' USA. I'd like to quote it for you now: "You really saved my bacon."

He replied immediately with:

> American poetry brings a tear to my eye. I hope you'll come prepared with more moving prose to share with me. Perhaps something along the lines of "Don't mess with Texas." Milwaukee is in Texas, isn't it?

I haul my stuff out of the pub, give the keys back to Eileen and Bill, and thank them profusely for allowing me to stay one more night. Eileen hugs me and says they might just pop up to the castle for a visit.

This time when I board the bus, I'm prepared with payment. I find a seat at the back where no one will trip over my luggage during the hour-long ride and look out the window.

The fact that this is my life is unbelievable. As devastated as I am that things didn't work out with Margaret, I was able to pivot. *That's growth,* I tell myself.

My nerves double with each passing minute. My thoughts bounce between *This is so exciting!* and *What the hell am I doing?* Is this dangerous? Is Finn conning me and I'll get out there, discover there is no castle, no job, and I'll be stuck in the middle of Nowhere, East Lothian, Scotland?

The more miles we pass, the more my thoughts shift into panic mode. Before I can totally spiral, I remind myself of the following:

1. If this is some cruel prank, I can just take the bus back.
2. Margaret did offer to pay for my flight home. Going home may not be ideal, but it won't kill me.

I change my focus to soaking up my surroundings. The sun is out today, showcasing the vibrant greens of fields and trees outside the city. We're in the countryside for miles. Out of habit, I reach for my phone and start taking photographs, intending to post them. I swipe, looking for all my regular apps before remembering that I deleted them all for a reason. I promised myself I wouldn't even look the entire summer. I don't want to torture myself. I have to be stronger than that.

We reach the town of Inveresk, where every building we

pass looks as though it could be the great-great-grandfather of the oldest building in Wisconsin. The bus pulls over on what I'm guessing is a main street in this quaint little town. I clamber off with my belongings in tow, get in a taxi, and ask the driver to take me to the castle.

"Sorry, love. They're closed today for the bank holiday."

"It's okay," I assure him, while trying to reassure myself. "They're expecting me."

He pulls off the main road onto a highway that traverses more countryside. I'm waiting to see the castle, but all I have a view of is lush trees. He turns, taking us to a black double gate with a gold coat of arms emblazoned on each one. The gate automatically opens. As he drives over a perilously narrow bridge, I take in the small cottage ahead that looks like a visitor's center. All around me are endless deciduous and coniferous trees, making the air smell sharp and fresh.

He parks in a lot and points to a path. "Follow that lane. Whoever's waiting for you will likely be up there."

The driver helps me with my luggage, I pay him and thank him profusely, silently praying that there really is someone up there who knows I'm coming. Otherwise, I'm stranded on private property. I imagine calling my parents from a Scottish prison, telling them I'm in for royal trespassing.

My suitcase bounces on the cobblestone. I have to

keep readjusting my backpack straps to stop the pinching in my muscles. When I reach the top, I begin to feel as though this will all be worth it. And I'm not even at the castle yet.

Ahead is a structure made of light gray stone; there are arches, a clock tower, and two spires on either side. Underneath the clock leans a familiar lanky form.

"There you are," Finn says, pushing off from the wall.

I'm too relieved to see a familiar face to give him any sass. I drop my bag and nearly hug him. He moves as if ready for it, but I duck away and make an awkward show of looking around. "Is this the castle?"

He snickers. "Hardly. Come on." He takes my suitcase from me and rolls it under one of the arches.

The grounds and the castle come into view. I don't know how to feel looking at it all because right now I feel *everything*. From what I can see, there are two large buildings with spires and turrets connected by a longer section. In front of the building, where we're now standing, is a parterre. I've never seen so many flower beds, and I definitely haven't seen them laid out in such ornate designs. The castle, the gardens, it's all more expansive than I imagined. I stop in my tracks to take it all in. I'd done some research last night when I couldn't sleep from nerves and excitement, but seeing an image that fits onto the screen of my phone versus seeing it in real life are two wildly different experiences.

"Do you like it?" he asks. To my surprise, he sounds like he sincerely wants to hear my opinion.

"Oh, I'm not that easily impressed. I *have* been to the stadium where the Green Bay Packers play, after all."

"I don't know what half of the things you've just said meant." He shakes his head. "Silly American. Shall we have a tour?"

"Please," I say, unable to stop myself from grinning.

He drops my bags off with a porter who appears out of nowhere and treats Finn with such deference, I almost laugh. I'm about to tease Finn about it, but he's just done me an enormous favor and my giddiness at living here for the summer is overpowering my desire to needle him. Instead, I say, "Okay, tour guide, tell me everything you know about this place, including how you had the pull to get me a job here so quickly."

"Old family friend," he says, sitting atop a short stone wall. Behind him are delicate purple flowers and shrubs shaped into perfect spheres. "As for everything I know about this place, you don't have that kind of time."

"I thought you said only tourists come here?"

He scratches his head and looks sheepish. "I'm a bit of a history nut, so I've read quite a bit."

"Give me the abbreviated version," I say as we begin walking. "I'm guessing I should know as much as possible if I'm going to be working here. Should I fake a Scottish accent?"

"Let's hear it." We stop and he crosses his arms, appraising me.

I pause, thinking back to an expression Bill said. I clear my throat. "Whit's fur ye'll no go by y—"

"*Stop,*" Finn says, laughing so hard he doubles over.

"Was that convincing?" I ask, unable to stop myself from laughing with him.

He takes me by the shoulders and looks me deep in the eyes. "American Hannah, I need you to promise me that you'll never, and I mean *never*, do that again. It was an assault on my ears and my patriotism."

"Ah dinnae ken," I say. "Now that I've started, I kind of—"

But Finn is walking away from me. With my short legs, I have to jog to catch up. He leads me down a few steps to a dirt path the color of terra-cotta. The path winds through the closest set of gardens.

"The castle was originally constructed for Kenneth MacAlpin," he begins. "Descendant of Kenneth the Hardy, the first king of Scotland. The British took it by force not long after as they claimed control of Scotland."

"How does that land with you, as an Englishman?" I ask, taking in the magenta foxgloves and bright yellow primroses. I'm tempted to pick them and make a bouquet. "Where are you at on the guilt scale?"

"Let's just say, I'm relieved Queen Victoria did some damage control there, thanks to her love of Scotland." He gestures at a stone bench in the middle of the floral labyrinth, and we sit. "And, truly, what's not to love?"

"I agree. But you've got to admit, royal families in general are problematic jackasses."

"Are they, now?" he asks, eyebrows raised.

"Unequivocally. Now, take me inside so I can see how those jackasses live."

Finn coughs and stands up with me. He leads me up a small set of stone steps to a path shaped like an hourglass. We take the side that leads toward the grand front door, which reminds me of a miniature drawbridge.

"Inveresk is one of many properties owned by the royal 'jackasses,' as you call them. While they're away, the castle is open to the public."

"Are they here now?" I ask, looking around. My Anglophilia doesn't extend beyond books and movies, and truth be told, I know almost nothing about the royal family.

"They're in the South of France, I believe," Finn says, "but the castle's closed to the public for the bank holiday, so your timing is perfect, really. You can get settled and do some training in the gift shop without the pressure of actual customers."

"Sorry," I say, confused. "Do you also work here or something? How do you know all this?"

He shrugs. "My family used to drag me here a lot on school holidays. They love visiting these old castles."

He pulls on a large iron ring, opening the door. "Hold on," I say. "Is it okay to just . . . go inside?" I look side to side, searching for someone in a uniform to grant us permission. I mean, you can't just walk into a castle, can you? But Finn is holding the door open for me, tapping his foot with exaggerated impatience, and so I step inside.

It's one thing to see opulence on a television or imagine it while reading a book. It's quite another to be face-to-face with it. Finn's saying something about how this is still a working estate with farmland, a den for the endangered grouse they protect, as well as Highland cattle and ponies. But all I can think is *How do people still live like this?* And I've only seen the entrance hall with its pine-paneled walls and an oak fireplace with ornate carvings. I make out some floral designs and shields and . . .

"Wait," I say, pointing to the frame. "Tell me that's not a series of unicorns."

"It's Scotland's national animal," Finn explains, as though that's totally normal. "If you mock it, I'll report you to the king."

I mime buttoning up my lips. Out of the corner of my eye, I see two maids peeking around a pillar down the hall. They scurry away. Oh god, are they going to call security on us? I debate pulling Finn back outside, but I really want to see more of the castle, so I decide to take the risk of an awkward interaction later. Finn seems like the type who can talk his way out of anything.

He shows me a cozy drawing room that's all creams, golds, pinks, and sage greens, then leads me through a red hallway that gives me *The Shining* vibes (the creepy sculptures of famous Scotsmen don't help the horror-movie factor). We end up in a dining room that has too many animal heads on the walls for my taste.

"It must be daunting to look in the eyes of the animal you're eating," I say, the taxidermic head of an elk staring deep into my soul.

"I'm more of a lover than a hunter," Finn agrees.

"I bet."

"I'm saving the best part of the castle for last," Finn says as we go back out to the hallway. He leads me to the most exquisite room I've ever seen.

"Oh, this is the best part of any home anywhere," I say, taking the castle library in. The tartan curtains let just enough light through to give the room a romantic, hazy feel. The carpet and furniture are plush, in rich blues and reds. Most importantly, there are books as far as the eye can see, all perfectly stacked, shelved, and organized. I let out a long sigh. "I'm in love."

"I'm flattered," Finn replies. "But I'm not really the 'settle down' type."

I give him a playful whack on the arm. "With this library, not with you."

"Noted."

"Can I . . . ?" We're hovering in the doorway, and I need

to step inside the room. *I need to.* "Will we get in trouble?"

"Only if we get caught," he says, making a big deal out of looking around to check if the coast is clear. He waves me in.

My first step is trepidatious, but as soon as I've crossed the threshold, there's no holding me back. I reach out and touch the glossy, mahogany desk that's probably worth more than my parents' house. I run a finger along the deep royal blue chaise longue, changing the grain of the velvet, and then I rub it back. Just as I'm wandering toward the first of the enormous bookcases, Finn clears his throat. "I should get you to the gift shop."

"Right, of course." *You're here to* work, I remind myself. A job that I was hired for without so much as an interview. I have to make a good first impression. I follow Finn back into the hallway.

"Beverly's waiting to train you. She's a bit of a dragon, so don't get on her bad side."

I nod, unsure whether he's joking about Beverly.

"Right. And you said you arranged a place for me to stay?"

"Yeah, most employees here live in town, but there was a free cottage in the servants' area, so they said you could stay there."

"'I am *excessively* fond of a cottage,'" I say, slipping into an English accent without thinking.

"Um, what?"

"Sorry, it's a quote from *Sense and Sensibility.*"

Finn clucks his tongue. "I thought we agreed you'd never attempt the accent again."

"You said I shouldn't try a *Scottish* accent!"

"Well, your English accent is somehow even worse. Though I didn't imagine that such a thing could be possible."

He flashes me a grin, then leads me back outside toward the clock-tower building, which I now see has a sign that says Gift Shop on it.

"How did you make all this happen?" I ask, realizing I never quite got clarification on that. "A family friend?"

He ignores the question and instead says, "Your luggage will be waiting for you at your cottage. Have Beverly show you the way after she's done with you."

"Okay, thank you," I say, slightly dazed by how much he seems to have done behind the scenes, how many strings he probably had to pull. The words don't feel like enough, so I reach out and touch his arm. He freezes. "I mean it. Thank you so much. This is insanely nice of you."

"Best of luck, American Hannah." Something flashes across his face, but I don't know him well enough to interpret it. And now I never will.

"If you ever want to come visit sometime, I'll buy you a thank-you gift from the shop."

He laughs, louder than I'm expecting. Then he raises his hand in farewell and disappears down the path toward the parking lot. Okay, time to switch into professional mode. I take a deep breath, roll my shoulders back, and walk into the gift shop. The first thing I see is an elderly woman in a pink cardigan, smiling at me like I've hung the moon. A dragon she is not.

The second thing I see are the mugs she's putting price tags on, each one featuring a different face. There's King Augustus, who I recognize. (The crown is a giveaway.) Queen Charlotte. And then their adult children, who I only recognize in context: Prince James, Princess . . . something or other. Two others. And then a few younger faces, who must be the grandchildren. A pretty redheaded girl I think is named Arabella. Or maybe Annabella? And then—wait, what?

The face on the next mug is very familiar, but not from the internet or magazine covers.

It's him, Finn.

Prince Finneas, the text reads.

It's a prank. It's got to be a prank. Beverly is probably Finn's grandmother or something and he had all the mugs made to mess with the naive American. I've just about convinced myself this is the case, when I look around and take in another piece of merchandise—the entire royal family on a gigantic serving platter: the king, the queen, all the others . . . and Finn.

Still a prank, still a prank, I think, as Beverly is introducing herself to me. How hard would it be to edit Finn into the photo of the royal family? And then print that on a platter—I glance at the display—about three dozen times. Okay, so an elaborate, expensive prank, but still doable . . . right?

Suddenly, I'm not so sure.

"Thank you so much for the opportunity," I hear myself tell Beverly. "I promise, you won't regret it." I try to smile, but I've just spotted a tin of candy called Prince Finneas's Sherbet Lemons. Could someone have gone to *this* much trouble to prank me? Maybe, but certainly not this quickly. Finn told me about the job less than twenty-four hours ago.

"Of course. His royal highness said you had loads of retail experience back in America," Beverly says kindly.

A lie, but that's the least of my problems right now.

She called Finn "his royal highness." No. No, this is not happening. And suddenly, memories I didn't realize I'd stored come rushing to the front of my mind. Magazine covers glimpsed in line at the grocery store, clickbait gossip columns I ignored but still registered. "Royal Gone Wild: Can Prince Finneas Be Tamed?" and "Prince Finneas Leaves Trail of Broken Hearts on Commonwealth Tour."

Oh my god, oh my god, oh my god. I've been hanging out with the damned prince of England, and I had absolutely no idea.

"Well. Let's get started." Beverly begins giving me a tour of the shop, where I see more and more trinkets with Finn's stupid face on them.

Oh my god, oh my god, oh my god. I referred to his whole family as "problematic jackasses."

Oh my god, oh my god, oh my god. I am the biggest fool on the planet and right now he's walking around the estate he *owns* and laughing at me.

I really am going to end up in prison here because the next time I see him I'm going to kill Prince Finneas.

6

Somehow, I manage to get through my training session with Beverly without bursting into flames of humiliation. It only gets worse when I realize the "servants' quarters" Finn's set me up in are my own private cottage. Yes, it's teeny tiny, but it's adorable and has a small kitchen (fully stocked with food), a bed, and a bathroom. And it's on the grounds of a castle, for crying out loud. I can almost hear Finn saying, *Who's the rapscallion now? I secured you a job and your own castle-dwelling cottage in less than twenty-four hours.* He's laughing at me. He's *been* laughing at me. Now that I think about it, back at the pub his friends were literally laughing at me because I clearly had no idea who he was.

I will never recover from this. I can practically hear Gigi's voice, screeching in horror and amusement at my total idiocy: *How can you recognize some random author on sight at a book festival and not know what the prince of England looks like, you total weirdo?*

I eschew sleep for staying up all night googling Finn. I need to know everything about him. I also need to find out the reasons why his friends have been tasked with keeping him out of trouble. As it turns out, those reasons are plentiful.

For his last birthday party, he leaked a story about a covert pool party. When the paparazzi showed up, he cannonballed into the pool—naked—giving them a full monty shot and then effectively ruining most of their equipment with the subsequent splash. And that's just the start. For the past six months, the paparazzi and gleefully shocked public haven't been able to get enough of him. Only a small percentage of the photographs have been royal family–approved appearances. The rest of them are of Prince Finneas clearly plastered out of his mind and/or making out with a random woman. He seemed to have a particularly wild phase after a breakup. I cover my face with my hands, realizing how easily that could've been me at The High Road Pub.

His most recent antics involve him dressing up in full drag as his great-great-great-grandmother, the esteemed Queen Henrietta II. The photos show him drunkenly vomiting into royal shrubbery.

I may not have known who he was, but my initial instincts about Finn were clearly correct: He is a walking red flag. No wonder his friends seemed so stressed out at the pub when they needed to escape. Someone must've spotted him and was ready to take a picture. Oh god. I was sitting with him. I could've ended up in all the gossip accounts too. I can't start college this fall looking like a side piece for a royal party boy.

I roll onto my stomach and continue scrolling through photos of the handsome devil (emphasis on "devil"). One thing is still bothering me. Knowing who he is and his reputation, I really can't understand why he helped me. If he's the no-good royal playboy he appears to be, why get me the job? Why set me up in this cottage? Why be so nice to me only to get literally nothing in return?

At some point, I manage to fall asleep, because I wake up to the sound of my alarm and the morning sun coming through the lace curtains. It takes me a minute to figure out where I am. My brain is foggy as I attempt to put context clues together. I look down at the small bed with the tartan quilt and pillows. I see a quaint breakfast nook a few feet away from me. When I sit up and look out the window, there's a castle.

Huh.

I obviously knew that none of this was a dream, but I did wonder. I have an excellent imagination, after all.

As I get dressed for my first day of work and make myself tea (I figure if I add enough milk and sugar, it might become palatable), I return to my original hypothesis: Finn is intrigued by me because I treat him like a civilian. He's probably also highly amused that I spent so much time with him without knowing who he is. I burn with shame, recalling how his friends laughed when I asked his name; how the maids in the castle spied on us from around the pillars.

Bastard.

I chug my tea, needing the caffeine after my sleepless night, and finish getting ready, hoping word about the clueless American hasn't spread.

The gift shop is a quick five-minute walk through perfectly manicured grounds. I arrive, expecting to see Beverly behind the counter. She was incredibly sweet and patient while training me yesterday. As it turns out, working a till is trickier when you don't have all the coin sizes and their corresponding values memorized. Instead of grandmotherly Beverly, I see a girl who's probably in her twenties. She's got bright orange hair that's shaved on the sides and styled up top. It's not a look many people could pull off, but she does.

"You must be the American," she says, looking up.

"I am. I'm Hannah," I say. Her Scottish brogue is so thick, it takes me a second to process what she's saying.

"I'm Caro. Can I hug you?" She steps forward. "I'm gonna hug you. You're the youngest person to work here in ages and I'm so relieved not to be stuck with an ancient relic all summer, eh?"

We hug. Orange and cinnamon fill my nose. She smells like Christmas, which endears me to her even more.

“Okay, we don’t open for another hour, and we’re supposed to be doing all the prep work,” Caro says, releasing me. She’s wearing a conservative button-up shirt and slacks that look out of place on her. Something tells me that’s not how she dresses on her own time. “But I came in early because everyone was talking about you in the group chat and I had to pick your brain and ask you, *How did you not know Finn is Prince Finneas?*” She laughs and it’s an adorable sound, despite it being at my expense. I redden.

“Who’s everyone and what are they saying?” I ask her, a little miserably.

“Oh, some of the house staff and the grounds crew and me—we all have a group chat on WhatsApp.” She pulls me in so I’m no longer standing at the entrance of the store. “Anyone we like is invited to be on it. I’ll get you added.”

“Will they mind?” It’s my first day and I’m certain people must already sense how unqualified I am for this job.

“Are you jokin’?” She claps her hands, and I see nearly every finger has a ring on it. “You’re a right celebrity around here. And if anyone gives you trouble, I’ll tell ’em off.”

Relief floods through me so potently, I nearly hug Caro again. I may have made a fool of myself, but I have one ally here. That’s enough to get me through for now.

She leans forward on the counter. “Be honest. When did you finally figure it out?”

“That Finn is . . . ?”

Caro nods.

I gesture to our surroundings. "When I walked in here and saw his face on everything."

Caro howls with laughter and slaps the counter.

I can't help it. I cover my face and put my head on the counter. "I'm an idiot."

"You're no eejit, you're just a foreigner." Caro pats my head. "Now, let's go round the store and tell me what you remember from Beverly training you yesterday."

The rest of the day goes by quickly, thanks to a steady stream of customers. Caro kindly takes the register, since I'm still getting a handle on what their money looks like. Instead, she puts me on wrapping up purchases and keeping the store tidy.

To my surprise, I enjoy the job—and Caro's company. Seeing Finn's face on notebooks, bells, shot glasses, commemorative plates, key chains, et cetera, et cetera? *That* I'm not enjoying.

When five o'clock comes, Caro invites me to get dinner with her in town, but I'm drained. My adrenaline, which has been surging for several days straight, is finally depleted. I'm glad my cottage came stocked with pantry staples because all I want to do is make myself something to eat and go to sleep.

"Please invite me out again," I tell her. "I'd really love to. I'm just—"

"Knackered?" she supplies.

"Maybe?" I say, which makes her laugh.

"It means you're exhausted," she says.

"Then, yes." I give her a hug and thank her for all her help.

When we lock up and she heads to the parking lot, I decide I'm not ready to hide in my tiny cottage. Not just yet. I don't have the energy to go out—or any idea how to get into town—but I do have enough for an evening walk. I start off on the path Finn led me down the day before by all the flower beds.

The summer sun is lowering, bit by bit, kissing each leaf and petal in the gardens. I inhale. I exhale. It's true—I am knackered. But my mind is running. I can't stop thinking about Finn and what stories I've missed about him and if he's known for helping tourists get jobs. Giving in to the compulsion, I sit on the nearest bench and pull out my phone. I enter his name into Google, scrolling past the articles I've already read.

"I knew it. You're obsessed with me," a voice says behind me.

I yell and throw my phone like it's an exploding grenade.

"You don't have to be so dramatic about it," Finn says, sauntering over to retrieve my phone from a patch of bell heather. He takes a look at the screen and mumbles things like, "Not my best angle . . . Ah, that's a good one. . . . Well, now, that one's just not even a little bit true. . . ."

I stand up and march over to him, palm out. "Can I have my phone back, please?"

"You can, but only if you promise next time you need to ogle me, you'll just ask." He gives me a performative twirl.

We stare each other down. I can't tell whether he's daring me to kiss him or to laugh. I do neither and show him my middle finger, which makes *him* laugh. I can't help but experience a small victory.

"How was your first day?" he asks, lowering himself onto the bench I just vacated.

"Fine." Even though I'm angry with him, I add, "Thanks again for the job."

"You can stop thanking me," he says. "Unless you want to thank me in a *different* way, in which case . . ." he trails off with a grin.

"I'll pass."

"You seem cross with me."

"Only because you're an ass."

He looks surprised, then shrugs. "Not the first time I've been called that. Usually it's pronounced 'erse,' or 'arse,' though." He puts up a hand. "That wasn't an invitation for you to do your horrendous Scottish impersonation again."

"With the exception of Caro, everyone in the castle is laughing behind my back," I tell him, irritated that he's trying to charm me instead of apologizing.

"Why's that?" he asks, wide-eyed with faux innocence.

"You know why." I stand up and point at him. "You didn't tell me who you are, which means I'm starting a new job with everyone thinking I'm a complete moron."

"I introduced myself within the first five minutes we met."

"Saying 'Hi, my name is Finn' is *not* the same thing as introducing yourself and you know it, so stop being deliberately obtuse. Yesterday I was afraid we'd get arrested for sneaking around the castle, and you *live here*."

"Hold on," he says, standing up. Unfortunately, he's got at least a foot of height on me and it's difficult to feel morally superior when you have to stand on your tiptoes to make a point. "Night one at the pub, I tried to give you clues."

"Oh yeah? Like what?"

"I mentioned that I'm supposed to stick to waltzes."

"Be a little vaguer next time," I say, aware I'm telling off a prince at his own castle and not really caring, because this prince deserves it. "I was so honest with you. I told you things I haven't told—"

I stop myself. Finn doesn't need to know that he's the only one I've ever admitted my plan about having Margaret MacIntyre call me a writer to. He doesn't need to know how vulnerable I was in that moment.

"I'm sorry," Finn says. This time he seems to mean it.

I really am on my tiptoes, so I lower my feet along with the volume of my voice. Flashes of the photographs I've seen from him over the years remind me that he's had to deal with a totally different life than I have. One devoid of privacy. Still, that doesn't give him the right to make me look stupid.

"You should be sorry," I say. "The very least you could've done is told me the second I got here."

"You don't have to forgive me right away," he says, his voice suddenly wicked. He licks his lips. "But I'd *love* the opportunity to make it up to you."

It doesn't matter how hot he is, he is 100 percent a *walking red flag*. And now he's an unrepentant one.

"Dream on, rapscallion," I tell him, furious. "I would *never* hook up with you. I'm not even interested in being your friend at this point." I turn to walk away.

"So you say, but I'm not the one doing the googling, Hannah," he calls after me. "I barely even know that you're from Milwaukee and appeared in your local paper when you were eight years old for winning a poetry contest."

Learning that he's been spying on me on the internet too makes me smirk. But I keep walking. Because he absolutely is trouble, and I have zero interest in becoming the conquest of someone who made me look like a fool.

7

I wake up with a start. It's still dark out and my heart is pounding like it's going to beat its way out of my chest. Yesterday when I started work, I was excited. But that was before I knew I was the laughingstock of Inveresk.

There's more. I've been so wrapped up in not going back home, saying yes to the first opportunity that allows me to stay here, I've forgotten what this summer was supposed to be. The romance of living at a castle has been sucked dry, thanks to Finn. So now I'm left with what? A job that has nothing to do with what I want out of life? This isn't going to make me a better writer. And I've seen what happens when you just blow along with the wind instead of pushing against the gales to get to where you want to be. I see it every day with my parents. As much as I love them, the last thing I want is to end up with a life like theirs.

I reach toward the nightstand until I grasp my phone.

When I open it up, I'm not googling the royal Finn. I will happily never google him again. No, this time I'm looking up things that are for my best interests.

Library internships Scotland

Scotland authors

I'm typing and scrolling and typing and scrolling, and by the time the sun is rising, peeking through my curtains, I'm still in the same place I was when I started: lying in bed with a job at a gift shop.

Yes, I'm at a castle, but I don't think scholarships and graduate programs in Creative Writing actually care about how impressive the location is when all you're doing is helping tourists buy sweaters that read I'm Scottish, We Dinnae Dae This Keep Calm Thing, followed by a graphic of a crown.

I swing my legs over the edge of the bed and try to give myself a pep talk. I'm in the middle of reminding myself that new experiences are almost always valuable in life and for writing inspiration when a new message pops up on my phone from Caro.

I added you to our Whatsapp gc. Come join!

It's a sweet gesture. Truth be told, I'm a little scared to dip into the group chat, especially knowing I'm the main cargo on the gossip train right now. I ignore the message for now and start getting ready for work. I'm looking forward to seeing Caro again—even if I am having a meltdown about what I'm doing here and my future.

On my short trek from the servants' cottages, I catch up to an older lady who's walking with purpose.

"The American," she says when she sees me.

"Hannah," I correct her as politely as I can.

"I'm Ethel. I'm the cook here at Inveresk. Don't you mind the havering about you and the prince. He's a right devil, always looking to get his hand caught in the cookie jar. But Beverly tells me you're a nice girl and Caro won't shut up about you."

"Oh." I'm taken aback. I guess not everyone is laughing at me. "Thank you."

"I told the staff to put some food in the kitchen of your cottage. I trust you're eating it."

"Yes, thank you," I say again.

"If you want a good stick-to-your-ribs dinner tonight, you come see me." She pats me on the arm and turns off for the castle while I head toward the gift shop. I'm about to thank her a third time, but she's already gone.

When I get to the shop, Caro is outside talking to two people standing near a golf cart. They both have work gloves in their hands.

"There she is," Caro says, waving to me. "Come meet the most brilliant people who work here." She indicates a woman who's probably in her late thirties, early forties, and has thick brown hair. "This is Leah. She's a riot. She's the supervisor for the grounds crew."

"I'm in charge of this lot," Leah says, indicating the man with blond hair, freckles, and bright blue eyes standing beside her.

"That's Duffie," Caro says. "He's funny too, just not as funny as Leah."

"It's not a competition," Duffie says. There's a strange vibe between him and Caro I can't quite put my finger on.

"It is when we're trying to get into Fringe," Caro tells him.

"Pipe dream," Leah says, shaking her head.

I have no idea what they're talking about, but I'm happy to meet new people who don't want to discuss the fact that I was duped by Prince Finneas.

"You should come to our next show," Caro says excitedly, taking me by the arms. "American comedy is so different, you might have some ideas on how we can improve."

"I'd love to." I have no idea what I'm promising, not that it matters. Caro's been so sweet and welcoming, I owe her several favors.

Leah and Duffie wave goodbye and get on their golf cart while I follow Caro inside, where there are several boxes sitting by the door. She tasks me with unpacking the new merchandise, including calendars of the royal family in their various estates. I scowl at every smiling photo of Finn before displaying them nicely on the shelf.

"What show did you invite me to?" I ask Caro, once she's finished setting up the register. "You, Leah, and Duffie do comedy?"

"Sketch comedy," Caro tells me. "You know, like *Saturday Night Live*."

"I actually went to a Groundlings show last year in LA." I think back to the senior class trip that also included a day in Disneyland and California Adventure, kayaking in Huntington Beach, and plenty of shenanigans in the hotel. It was also the place where I first said "I love you" to . . . I shake the memory from my mind. That doesn't matter.

"The Groundlings?" Caro says, clapping her hands. "That's brilliant."

Thinking about the trip makes me homesick, but not for home. More for a feeling of belonging. It's been months since I've experienced it.

"What's wrong?" Caro kneels down beside me, where I'm unpacking a box of tea towels featuring an artist's rendering of Inveresk Castle.

"Nothing," I tell her. "Just some bad memories of a boy who broke my heart."

"Tell me about it," she says, only instead of waiting for me to answer, she goes on her own tirade. "That gadge, Duffie? He and I were in a situationship for the better part of last year. I finally told him, 'Duff, my head's mince. Are we something or are we nothing?'"

"What did he say?" I fold a tea towel and add it to a pile.

I knew there was something going on between the two of them.

"The lad started *crying*. He's thirty years old and instead of making a decision, he turned on the waterworks."

"What?" I cover my mouth with my hand. "What are you supposed to do with that?"

Caro shrugs. "Exactly. Outside of our comedy troupe, we stopped talking. Eventually it stopped being awkward and we went back to being pals."

"That's impressive you two can still work together, never mind be friends. I can't imagine ever being friends with my ex," I tell her.

"It's not for the faint of heart, that's for sure." She points to some bookmarks that have the queen's face on them. "Can you fix them tassels? They're all fankled."

As I detangle the tassels, I silently wish I could fix my fankled life, while I'm at it.

Caro tells me she's got sketch rehearsal tonight but wants to take me into town another time after work. I readily agree. I'm not looking forward to another evening alone with my thoughts. Those guys can be real bampots, as they say here. I'm locking up the shop when Finn approaches.

"How was your day?" he asks.

"You just love to sneak up on me, don't you?" I put the keys to the shop in my purse.

"Sneak up?" He chuckles. "I walked towards you in your eyeline. I'd be the worst burglar."

"The worst," I agree. I'm so torn between my anger at him and not wanting to be alone right now. I stand, rooted to the spot, and wait for him to say something to make me run away or follow him.

"Plans?" he asks.

"Ethel promised me food if I come by the kitchen." I look out into the bright blue sky, the trees sheltering me from real life. I may be feigning nonchalance, but I've never felt so lost. "So. I've got that going for me."

"Brilliant. Let's go get some of Ethel's cooking and then I can finish giving you the tour."

"If the tour includes your bedroom, you can skip it," I tell him, still not trusting him one bit.

He brings a hand to his chest as though he's been scandalized. "Hannah. Here we speak to the royal family with a little more decorum."

I can't help it. I laugh. "Sorry, Your Highness."

"Forgiven. Now, let's go sneak up on Ethel and give her a scare."

"Don't you dare. She looks like she's eighty."

"You underestimate her. She's at least a hundred and three."

We walk in silence toward the castle. He opens an ancient turquoise door that leads straight to the kitchen. The tiled floor is in a black-and-white checkerboard pattern.

Copper pots and pans line and hang down from a tall shelf that runs the perimeter of the room. There are stainless steel workstations as well as an island with a marble top with barstools around it. In the middle of it all is Ethel, her hair in a bonnet, apron on, methodically stirring a pot of stew.

"I knew I could tempt you," Ethel says to me. She gives Finn a frown. "I don't remember inviting you, stickler."

"You wound me, Ethel," Finn says, giving her a kiss on the cheek. "Do you really want to leave me to cook for myself? I'll get scurvy."

Ethel ladles up two bowls of aromatic stew and serves us warm rolls, fresh from the oven, to go with it.

"We can eat in the dining room, if you'd like," Finn says to me.

Something about his tone leads me to believe that's not his first choice. I glance at Ethel, who gives a slight shake of her head.

"Can we eat here?" I point to the stools at the island.

Ethel smiles approvingly at my suggestion, though I'm not sure whether it's because this is what Finn prefers, or she wants to keep an eye on us.

While we eat, Finn asks me about my life back in Milwaukee.

"Tell me everything," he says. "Do you have any siblings? Have you ever worn one of those cheese hats to an American football game—"

"Were you googling Wisconsin too?" I interrupt, but he ignores me.

"Are your parents the types of Americans who say things like 'that's rad' or 'working hard or hardly working'?"

"Let me stop you right there." I put down my soup spoon. "I'm an only child; I have never worn a Cheesehead; I've never in my life heard anyone, American or otherwise, say, 'that's rad'; and my parents are too busy complaining about each other to toss out folksy idioms like 'working hard or hardly working.'"

"Fine, then, what sorts of holidays does your non-folksy family of three take?" He's unknowingly hit upon my favorite thing about my dysfunctional family, which is our trips to Pike County. "Ah, we've found something you like," Finn says approvingly. "It's written all over your face."

I really am torn between my annoyance at his very existence and this weird type of homesickness I haven't been able to shake. With Ethel here to swat Finn with a wooden spoon should he act up (something tells me she wouldn't hesitate, prince or not), I give in and speak. "My family drives to southern Illinois every summer. It's the only time my parents' arguing is at a minimum."

My mind conjures images of driving in the car, listening to boy bands, all three of us singing along.

"And what's in southern Illinois?" he asks.

"A log cabin that's been turned into a bed-and-breakfast," I say, finally pinpointing that homesick feeling.

The trip to Pike County is what I'm missing. The familiarity, the coziness. "We roast marshmallows at night at the outdoor firepit, read books until it's time for bed. During the day we ride ATVs on these endless trails, we have picnics and go bird-watching. . . . There's a horse ranch, but I've always been too scared to go riding."

"You're scared of horses?" Finn asks in surprise.

I take my last bite of stew and pretend not to hear him.

"Hannah . . ."

"Fine," I say, crossing my arms. "Yes, I'm scared of horses. For the same reason I'm scared of whales and elephants and—" I stop when I realize Finn is trying not to laugh at me. Glaring at him, I fling my arms wide in a *look at me* gesture. "What? They're too big!"

This only makes the laughter break through his pursed lips. I'm about to get angry with him when Ethel comes by and swats him with a tea towel. I knew she was on my side.

"Mind your manners," she says to the literal prince of England. Ethel might be my new hero.

In order to regain some dignity, I straighten up and change the subject. "What about you? Where did you vacation growing up?"

"I spent most of my summers here," he tells me. "The school year was obviously spent in England. Winters were for skiing in Switzerland, but summers? Those were for playing in the forest and—you're going to hate this—riding."

"Madness."

"We have tiny Highland ponies." He gestures out the window. "They're the perfect size for you."

"I could ride an actual horse," I tell him just to shut him up, even though the thought makes my stomach drop into my knees.

"Oh?"

"Yep," I lie. "No problem."

"Well, let's go see, shall we?"

"What? Now?"

He stands and reaches his hand out to help me up. "No time like the present. Time to let out your inner American cowgirl."

8

We pass a paddock with a wire fence. On the other side are some of the cutest creatures I've ever seen—the same Highland cows that made up the knockers on Margaret MacIntyre's front door.

"Oh my god, *these cows.* I've never seen one in real life," I coo, approaching the fence. They're a brown so warm they're almost orange. Their horns are on the dramatic side, but I don't mind. The best thing about these babies is they have amazing uneven bangs hanging over their eyes. "Do you ever want to pull their hair up and put it in a bow so they can see better?"

"Now you're really stalling." Finn drags me away from the cows toward the stables. "Why aren't cows scary? They're big."

"Those babies are gentle, I can tell. Besides, I'm not trying to hop on one. I just want to style their hair."

"If you get on a horse today, I promise to let you style the cows all you want."

"How about if I just watch *you* ride a horse and cheer you on?"

"Rosie is very sweet. Not scary at all."

"Anything that can kill you by stepping on you is scary," I shoot back. "What time is it anyway? Isn't it too late to go riding? Probably the horses want to go to bed soon."

"So thoughtful of you to worry about Rosie's bedtime," Finn says wryly, "but we have at least two more hours of broad daylight."

"Are you sure?" I stop walking and pull out my phone. "I should slowly google it and find out." But when my screen lights up, I see a text from Gigi.

I know you're avoiding me, but I still can't believe you left for Scotland without even talking to me.

My hand is shaking as I darken the screen and put my phone back in my small crossbody bag. Finn stares at me questioningly but thankfully doesn't say a word. We start walking again. We're so close, I can hear the horses now. The smell of hay fills my nostrils as we approach the stables. The structure is made from the same light gray granite ashlar as the rest of the castle. Outside, tied up, is an adorable spotted gray pony not much bigger than a golden retriever, contentedly chewing on some hay. “Please tell me I get to ride that one.”

“You don’t.”

While Finn chats amiably with the stable hand and tells him to go enjoy a break, my fear grows and the text from Gigi plays on repeat in my head. *I know you’re avoiding me, but I still can’t believe you left for Scotland without even talking to me.* I squeeze my eyes shut, shame and fury lighting up behind my lids. Life is unfair. Everything is unfair. And I don’t want to ride a stupid horse.

Finn returns to me and we’re alone.

“Why do *you* get to make all the rules?” I say, crossing my arms. It’s immature, but I don’t care. I’m pissed. About everything. And now that two-thousand-pound animals are involved, we’re going to talk about it.

“I beg your pardon?” Finn says, clearly bewildered by my sudden shift in tone.

“I know you think I’m over what you did, but I’m not. Maybe you didn’t need to tell me who you were at the pub—not when I figured we’d never see each other again. But the next day?” I say, “That next day when you came by and told me you ‘had connections’ at the castle and could get me a job? Not telling me then was a real dick move.”

“I know.” He certainly doesn’t sound repentant. “Is this really what you’re upset about?”

I know you’re avoiding me, but I still can’t believe you left for Scotland without even talking to me.

"What are you talking about? Of course I'm upset about it," I snap. "I'm also upset that Margaret, the woman who was my hero and the person I planned my summer *and* my life around 'buggered off,' as you Brits say, with some dude to another country. That is so messed up."

"It is." He's not arguing with me, he's agreeing with me, and it's only making me feel worse.

"*And now you're going to make me ride a horse*," I cry. "You're keeping me here for your own amusement and this will amuse you."

"I—"

"That's what this is, isn't it?" The idea is becoming clearer to me. Saying it out loud makes it ring true. And it really is coming out *loud*. "You invited me here to either sleep with me or to laugh at me. Well, both scenarios suck for me!"

It takes Finn a moment to recover from my tirade. When he does, he clears his throat. "First of all, if we had sex, I can promise it would *not* suck for you. Not unless that's what you requested," he adds with a wink.

I let out a frustrated growl and whip around to walk back to my cottage, but he takes me by the arm and spins me back to face him.

"Did it occur to you," he says, his voice suddenly weary, "that I invited you here because I'm desperately and pathetically lonely?"

I open my mouth, but nothing comes out.

"Yes, I know," he says, throwing his head back. "The poor little prince has no one to play with. Well, that author may have 'buggered off' on you, but my entire family buggered off on me as a punishment. I humiliated them in the press and so they put me in a time-out here while they're all spending weeks together in the South of France, pretending I don't exist. We can debate whether I deserve the treatment, it's still—"

"What about your friends?" I interrupt him because I'm starting to feel an inkling of pity, and I don't want to. "Callum and Mhairi and Bethany? They're here for you."

"Oh yes, they love having to babysit me. They love spending their twenties running from camera-happy people and paparazzi—who are not technically people, by the way." He takes a breath. "They love hiding in their summer flat in Edinburgh with me, getting drunk in a living room instead of going out dancing. The other night, whilst hiding in the flat, we turned on the television and played a game called 'Anytime something happens, take a drink.' Thrilling it was not."

I remember how excited the three of them got when a song they liked came on at the pub, how happy they seemed just to be out. Didn't Mhairi say something about wanting the chance to finally hook up with someone? Clearly I'm not the only one whose summer plans were derailed.

"They seem to really care about you, though," I point out. "They wouldn't do all that if they didn't love you."

"You're right. They've sacrificed a lot for me during the course of our friendship, and right now I'm repaying them by doing what I'm supposed to: staying at Inveresk full-time."

"You weren't supposed to be in Edinburgh at all," I say, putting everything together. That's why they all freaked out when someone tried to take a picture of Finn—not necessarily because he was getting into trouble, but because he was off castle grounds.

"I wasn't. Now I'm back here, behaving myself, which gives Bethany, Callum, and Mhairi time to actually enjoy their youth—something I'm forbidden from doing."

"Oh." It isn't enough, but I don't know what else to say while I'm still processing everything.

The atmosphere begins to thaw as I look at things from his perspective. Most people get to make stupid choices in their youth and not have those choices plastered on papers and the internet for the entire world to judge. Most people get to move through the world without moving under a spotlight. It's not like Finn chose any of this—he was born into it.

"I'm sorry for yelling at you," I say, then add, "even if what I said was valid."

There's a pause. "I wasn't trying to use you for my own entertainment," Finn says quietly. "I just didn't want to be here by myself, and you needed a job. The arrangement seemed to be beneficial for both of us." He sighs. "If this job isn't the right fit, if you don't want to spend the summer at Inveresk—or if you feel you should be back in America—I can help with travel arrangements."

I've made plenty of assumptions about Finn, but they've largely been based on media headlines. I'm starting to see there's more going on underneath the surface of his party boy facade.

"I don't want to leave the castle or the job," I tell him. *Not just yet anyway.* "But I do want to leave these stables. So. Good talk."

"Not so fast, coward. Before you go, at least come and *meet* Rosie."

Meeting a horse is much different than jumping on her back and galloping to my doom. It's an interesting compromise.

"Rosie's currently tied up? She can't trample me?"

"Rosie would *never* trample you," Finn promises. "She's in her stall anyway."

My curiosity gets the better of me and I follow him inside. The smell of horses and hay becomes overpowering, though not in an unpleasant way. Stalls line each side of the narrow walkway, each affixed with a brass plaque bearing the occupant's name. Chester. Frodo. Wellington. As we pass, a few curious heads emerge to watch us, or even try to nuzzle our arms. I keep mine firmly affixed to my sides.

As we approach Rosie's stall, she extends her neck over

the top and whickers in greeting. It's almost—*almost*—kinda cute. "Hello there, gorgeous girl," Finn murmurs, scratching her behind the ears. She closes her eyes and stretches forward, as if guiding him to a particularly itchy spot.

Her coat is copper, nearly the same color as Finn's hair, and there's a strip of white down her nose that matches the stripes on her legs I can just glimpse through the bars. She looks like she's wearing knee socks.

"She's very pretty," I admit. "For a potential murderer."

At the sound of my voice, Rosie's head turns. Her eyes are large and dark and captivating. I swear she sees all the way through me.

"You can pet her," Finn says. "She's gentle, I promise."

I lift up a hand and tentatively stroke her nose.

Finn chuckles. "You're petting the air, American Hannah. You'll have to get a bit closer than that."

Rosie's holding very still, and I swear she nods at me in encouragement. I take half a step closer and reach my hand out farther until it connects with her velvety muzzle. She pushes her nose up into my hand and I immediately pull away.

"That means she likes you," Finn says. "She's being friendly. Try again."

I extend my hand a third time. When she pushes back, I don't flinch.

"Do you want to try riding her?" Finn asks. "We can start out nice and easy. I'll hold on to her reins while you sit on the saddle, and we'll just walk around a little."

"You promise you'll keep hold of her?" I ask, my voice wavering. "You promise we'll just walk around slowly and the second I get scared I can get off?"

"I promise. So are you in?"

To my own surprise and before I can even properly think about it, I nod. *Yes.*

"Brilliant." Finn ducks into Rosie's stall, slips a halter over her head, and leads her into the aisle. "These are called crossties," he explains, hooking two rope things to her halter.

Rosie really does seem gentle. Beyond that, *Finn* is being gentle. With the two of them, I might feel safe. Possibly. Hopefully.

I watch as Finn runs a brush over her already-shining coat. There's something soothing about it, like an ASMR video. The soft sounds, the repetitive motion. A groom scurries over and offers to help, but Finn politely turns him away. "Granny's policy," Finn explains. "You can't just show up for the fun bits. If you're going to ride, you have to take care of the horse as well."

He disappears for a moment, then returns with a saddle in his arms and a bridle draped over his shoulder. He looks more handsome than he has all day, like he's stepped out of a Ralph Lauren ad. I try not to stare as he finishes tacking Rosie up, but I can't help but be impressed by his smooth confidence.

Finn leads Rosie outside and motions for me to follow by his side. "Never walk behind a horse. Even one as sweet as Rosie." He gestures at a set of steps a few yards ahead. "Go stand on the mounting block, and I'll bring her round."

My legs tremble as I climb the steps, and it's almost a relief to have something to hold on to when Finn leads Rosie around. "Hold on to the saddle here," Finn says, "then place your left food in the stirrup and swing your right leg over."

It takes me a few tries, but then I'm on. I've done it. I'm on a horse!

"Just take a few deep breaths," Finn instructs. "All you need to do is stay relaxed. I'll handle the rest." He clucks to Rosie, who begins to walk slowly at his side, like a dog who's been trained to heel. I do as I'm told, and after a few breaths, feel my hips begin to sway in time with Rosie's steps. "You're doing well," Finn says.

The sun is just starting to set. The clouds are highlighted with pinks and oranges, the trees and grass turning different shades of green. It's so beautiful, I almost forget to be nervous.

Finn leads Rosie down a dirt path that runs parallel to the paddock, then veers off toward a meadow bordered with trees. For a moment, I wonder what it'd feel like to go faster. To trot or even gallop, feeling the wind stream past my face as Rosie's hooves fly across the ground.

"You don't have much of a poker face," Finn says after a few minutes.

"What do you mean?" I ask.

"I can tell you're enjoying yourself."

"Rosie and I have bonded," I say. "You and I, on the other hand?"

"Yes, I know," he says with a smile. "No bonding between you and me. I'm a rapscallion, after all."

"Exactly."

We walk on in companionable silence for a bit until the sky darkens, and we agree it's time to head back.

"Next time we'll both be on horses," Finn says. "Then you'll get to see a lot more of the grounds."

"Next time?" I raise my eyebrows.

"Next time." Finn raises his eyebrows back at me. "Don't pretend you don't want to go riding again."

"Fine. But I swear to god, if you say, 'I told you so,' I'll push you in a pile of hay."

"Now, that could be fun. Nothing I love more than a roll in the hay." *Damn*, I think. *Walked right into that one.* "But for now, why don't you focus on holding the reins?" He flips the leather straps over Rosie's head and shows me how to grasp them between my middle finger and ring finger, placing my thumb on top. "Now give her a little squeeze with your calves."

"She won't run away with me?"

"Definitely not. I'll be right here the whole time."

I trust him, I realize. "Okay." I squeeze my calves and Rosie walks forward. . . . I squeal. "I'm riding a horse in Scotland!"

"That you are, American Hannah."

When we arrive back at the stable, Rose stops without my telling her to. I guess she knows the drill. But I have no idea how to get off. Suddenly, I no longer feel safe. I'm way too high up. I'm certain that this is how I die: trying to get off a horse.

"Just swing your leg back over," Finn says patiently.

I shake my head. "That's okay. I'll just stay up here. Rosie and I will have a sleepover."

"Lucky Rosie." Finn comes over next to the horse, his hand on my leg. "Lean forward and swing your right leg over. I promise I'll catch you."

Obviously sleeping here isn't really an option. Besides, Finn's hand is so warm on my thigh, the feeling is spreading low in my belly. There are goose bumps forming on my arms I don't want him to clock, or he'll never let me hear the end of it.

As he instructed, I swing my leg over, and just as he said he would, he catches me.

His hands go from my hips to my waist to under my arms as I dismount. My feet touch the ground, but neither one of us lets go. My back is pressed against his chest, and I can feel his breath on my neck. Every molecule I'm made of is buzzing. . . .

"Ahem." An abrasive throat clear pours cold water on whatever was happening between us, and we leap apart.

Standing in the entryway of the stables is a severe-looking woman with gray-streaked hair that's pulled back from her face. The expression of disapproval she's giving us immediately makes me blush.

"Tina," Finn says, taking the saddle off Rosie. "What a lovely surprise. How's your day been?"

"I'm about to ring the king and queen to give them my nightly report," she says curtly. She eyes me and I swear the temperature in here drops twenty degrees. "Shall I tell them about our new guest?"

"This is Hannah," Finn says. Once Rosie's back in her stable, Finn puts a hand on my lower back to guide me toward a woman who scares me more than every horse in here. "Hannah, this is my prison warden—sorry, the *deputy chief of staff*—Tina."

"It's a pleasure to meet you." I curtsy because, I don't know, I'm a terrified idiot, which makes Finn choke on a small laugh and Tina regard me with even more derision.

"Hannah is working at the gift shop with Caro for the summer. Beverly has given her rave reviews thus far."

"I see," Tina replies coolly, clearly irritated this is the first she's hearing about me.

I'm expecting Tina to leave, to go have her phone call with the king and queen, but she stays put. It occurs to me that I'm supposed to be the one who leaves.

It's probably for the best. That moment Finn and I just had felt flammable, and my life is already on fire in so many ways.

"It's a pleasure," I say to Tina, repeating myself, and

much to my horror, I curtsy again. This time, Finn doesn't laugh.

"Good night," Tina says, effectively excusing me.

"Good night," I reply. I turn back to Finn. He's surprising me in so many ways, I don't know what to say or how to feel about him anymore. I settle on, "Thanks for the riding lesson."

As soon as I'm sure I'm out of sight, the grin I've been holding back spreads across my face.

9

"That fine bone china teacup is beautiful," I say to the first Americans I've encountered since landing in Scotland.

"I'm obsessed," the woman says. She can't stop looking at everything in the shop, even though her male counterpart seems ready to leave.

I lean forward. "Did you see the whole tea set? It comes with a pot and two cups—and it doesn't cost that much more."

"*No*," the woman says. I lead her to it. She also snags a box of Royal Blend Tea while she's there.

I check out her purchase (I'm much more confident on the register now that I've been working here a week), carefully wrap the tea set, all while chatting amiably with her. Once they leave and another rush of customers funnels out, Beverly approaches.

"I've been watching you, bonny," she says, a twinkle in

her eye. “You’re a natural with the customers and you upsell nearly everyone.”

“I worked retail all through high school,” I tell her. “And I love pretty much everything in here, so it makes the job easy.”

She pats my hand and walks away to talk to Caro about a new display. I feel a burst of pride. Maybe this is a good fit. No, it’s not what I expected my summer to look like, but it’s better than staying home, avoiding my best friend, and playing referee to my parents.

“You lasses go have a piece,” Beverly says to us, looking at one of the many clocks in the store. “I’ll keep an eye out here. Another tour won’t be out for forty-five minutes. Take advantage of the quiet—and the braw day.”

“What’s a piece?” I whisper to Caro as we’re leaving.

“A sandwich,” Caro tells me. She’s been my translator, although half the time I’m asking her what *she’s* saying. Caro’s carrying a blanket so we can picnic under the trees. She suggested we eat our lunches together whenever Beverly is around to keep an eye on the store, which I’m happy to do. I’d truly rather not be alone with my thoughts. Not when they keep veering off course and to that moment in the stable with Finn. I haven’t seen him since then. Granted, it’s only been a couple of days, but that’s weird when you live on the same estate.

Caro and I get settled on the blanket with the sandwiches we brought.

"How's your sketch troupe going?" I ask her.

"Brilliant," she enthuses, her orange hair falling into her eyes. It reminds me a bit of the cute bangs on a Highland cow. "Leah wrote this hysterical thing about—okay, I won't ruin it in case you come to our next show—"

"I'll definitely come," I tell her. From what Caro has said, Leah's like a Scottish Paula Pell when it comes to comedy writing, and I'm invested. "Are things okay between you and Duffie?"

Caro drops her sandwich into her lap and covers her face.

"Caro . . ." I say. "What did you do?"

"It was only a winch in a moment of weakness," she says, dramatically flailing her arms out. "And then it turned into ripping each other's clothes off in his flat."

"*Caro*," I say, but I'm laughing. "You just can't quit him."

"I can't," she says with a shake of her head. "Have you ever had a boy like that? One you just couldn't resist?"

"Nope," I say with confidence, swatting away a memory of the stable scene with Finn for the second time.

We fall quiet. A light wind rustles through the trees. Birds are singing various tunes. It's perfect. In this place, in this moment, I'm content, which immediately fills me with guilt. I'm supposed to be focusing on my career, my future this summer, not chilling at a castle.

"Hey, Caro?" I sit up and cross my legs. Even though what she does is different, she's still a creative and seems to be centered. Focused. "What do you do when you've got a plan that falls through? Like, if you have a goal with your comedy troupe and something happens to throw you off course?"

"Aw, hen, that's my life. Things rarely go the way I plan them." Caro shrugs, an ease to her countenance. "I switch gears. I keep my goals the same and I just change how I get there."

Caro's words sink in. My situation's changed, but my goals haven't, I remind myself. I can still write this summer. In fact, not being Margaret's assistant will allow me more time to focus on my own projects. I think back to when Margaret told me that she doesn't chase the muses—the muses chase her. If I finish a manuscript while I'm here, I'll be able to tell myself at the end of this trip that I'm a writer.

Come find me, muses.

But I can't focus. Because down in the parterre, I can see Finn jogging around the flower beds. He's wearing shorts, running shoes, and . . . that's it. I've never seen him shirtless before and good lord does that man have a body.

"What is he doing out here?" Caro says.

Fixated on the view before me, I barely hear her. "Oh, is he supposed to stay inside?" I say vaguely.

"When tours are going on, aye. Normally, we shut them down altogether when the family's here, but since Prince Finneas is about for the summer, the tours are truncated a wee bit. He's supposed to stay tucked away, not running around half scud."

"Huh," I say. He looks *really* good.

"Close your mouth already," Caro says with a laugh. She knocks her foot against mine.

"I . . ." I rack my brain for an excuse as to why I was just ogling the prince of England and come up with nothing. "I wasn't looking at him, I was admiring the flowers."

"That's the daftest excuse I've ever heard," she squeals. "You're blushing."

"No, I'm not," I lie, feeling the heat on my cheeks. I remember how close I was to kissing him and am sure I turn redder. "I told you when I started working with you that Finn and I are barely even friends. I barely know him." I can't stop saying the word "barely." I can't stop looking at his bare chest.

"You liar. You *fancy* him. All this talk about, 'Oh, we're just mates, we met in a pub, and he helped me out after I lost my job,' that's all shite because you *fancy him*."

She's shaking my leg with her hand now and I know I'm bright red now, which is fully incriminating even though I swear I *do not like Finn*. That would not only be ridiculous, that'd be full-throttled batshit crazy.

"Okay," I finally say, putting my hand up in protest. "I will admit, he looks good half naked. I have eyes, okay? And an ill-advised attraction to men. Sue me."

"Uh-huh . . ." Caro says, her eyes dancing.

"*However*, I am not masochistic enough to like a playboy prince who spends his off-hours getting plastered and making out with random socialites. I mean, I've got more dignity than that."

The electricity I experienced when Finn and I had our hands on each other in the stables shoots through me again, so I stand up and sit back down, this time with my back to him.

"See? I'm not looking at him," I say. "I'm so disgusted with his personality, I don't even want to look at his hot body."

"It's okay to admit the man's got a rig," Caro says with a sigh. "But he's no Duffie."

I laugh. One of us is definitely delusional here, and it isn't me.

10

I decide to finally join the WhatsApp group chat, if only because I figure my presence will curb any rumors Caro might start about my feelings for Finn. My sense is she wouldn't do that, but I need to make sure. I've learned the hard way that people aren't always what they seem.

"Ethel's in the group?" I ask, scrolling through.

"Oh aye. She always has loads to say." Caro points out some of the other group-chat members I haven't met yet.

"Tina's not in here, right?" I ask.

"Are you mad?" Caro gives me a look. "When did you meet Tina? More importantly, how did you survive?"

"Finn was giving me a riding lesson the other night," I say without thinking. "I promise you, there's nothing going on between Finn and me. For either of us."

I don't allow myself to think of the time he held my hands in the pub and told me I'm a writer. I try to deny how sweet he was with me when I was riding Rosie. But all the thoughts I'm attempting to ignore come crashing in when, five minutes until closing, we get one last customer.

Finn's dressed in navy-blue slacks and a white button-up shirt. He's rolled up his sleeves. His copper hair is mussed in a flattering way, and his eyes flicker with mischief the second they lock with mine.

So much for convincing Caro there's nothing going on between us. Even though there really isn't, his appearance at the shop is damning evidence.

"Sorry, sir," I say. "We're closing. You'd best find somewhere else to purchase your narcissistic treasures."

"She doesn't mean that, of course you're welcome here anytime. Obviously, Your Majesty," Caro stammers. Quietly and out of the side of her mouth, she hisses, "Oh my god, Hannah, I know you're American, but what are you doing?"

However, Finn seems amused by my insolence and is now wandering the store as though he's shopping: picking up biographies about his parents and flipping through them while *tsk*ing and saying things like "patently untrue."

Caro looks like she's about to wet herself from nerves, so I tell her I'll lock up tonight if she wants to head out.

"Aye, please, get me out of here," she says, before adding, "don't do anything I wouldn't do."

I roll my eyes and push her out the door. When I turn back to my so-called customer, he's holding up a mug with his own face on it.

"He's certainly a handsome bastard. You must sell loads of these."

"Sadly, no. Our customers would all rather drink out of the corgi mug. It's much easier on the eyes."

"Come on, then," he says, smirking at me. "What's the most popular item in here?"

I pick up the bobblehead-doll version of him. "This little guy. I think people like to smack his head more than they like to watch it wobble, though."

To prove my point, I flick it with my thumb and index finger. "Ah. So satisfying."

"You're such a pain the arse, I don't know why I put up with you," he says with a long-suffering sigh.

"I don't recall ever asking you to."

"Alas, I'm a glutton for punishment. And so here I am to save you from boredom and take you out."

"You mean save yourself from boredom." Warning bells at the prospect of spending time alone with him ring loud and clear. I'm not in enough denial to pretend we don't have chemistry, and I'm still convinced if I hooked up with him in a moment of weakness, he would replace me with another toy. Now that I'm settled into castle life, I don't want to leave.

I lean against the counter and level him with a look. "I thought I made myself abundantly clear that I have no interest in you romantically."

My rebuff doesn't even faze him.

"I don't want to take you out on a date, you goose." He picks up a pamphlet touting all the amazing things you can see at the castle and bops me on the top of the head with it. "I need to get out of this place before I go mad and I'm using you as an excuse. I told the warden that American Hannah hasn't even been to Musselburgh yet." He pauses. "You haven't yet, right? I'm not looking to outright lie, just bend the truth."

I shake my head. "I haven't, no. Hey, who's the warden?"

"You met her after you bravely rode a horse." He gives me a winning smile. "Remember that sweet little crumpet named Tina?"

I shudder. "She's terrifying."

"She's all bark and no bite. Now, are you coming with me or do I need to find another foreigner to use as a cover story?"

I mentally weigh the pros and cons. It *would* be nice to see more of the country.

"Hannah . . . ?" His eyes are daring me, and that's what clinches it.

"Fine. I'll go. But I'm paying my own way, and you're not allowed to find a single excuse to touch me." I pull myself as tall as I can so he knows I'm serious.

"*I'll* pay," he counters, "and I'll only touch you if you beg me to."

"In your dreams."

"Now, how did you know about that? Have you been peeking at my dream journal?"

I ignore him under the guise of locking up. Upon exiting the shop, I note that the beautiful blue sky I enjoyed during my lunch hour has since clouded over, threatening rain. Back home, when the clouds looked like this, Gigi would say, *Look, the sky's constipated.* I nearly smile at the memory as we walk.

"What just happened in that head of yours?" Finn asks, leading me into the carriage house that's been converted to a garage for stupidly expensive cars.

"Nothing," I lie. "Now. Which one are we taking and can I drive?"

"We'll take the least ostentatious," he says, unlocking a Rolls-Royce Cullinan.

"Yes, so subtle." I head toward the driver's side door before remembering they drive on the opposite side, and I've just gotten in the passenger seat. Finn is clearly amused by my miscalculation.

"It's not my fault you all are backwards," I say with a scowl. I can't sulk for long, because the supple leather is cradling me in a way that makes me want to propose to this car.

"Ah, yes. We're the backwards ones, you metric-resisting fool." The engine roars to life and he shushes it. Slowly, he pulls out and heads down the road. To my surprise, he spends the first few miles crawling along well under the speed limit.

"Finn," I say eventually. "Have you ever been behind a wheel before? I really am happy to drive if you need me—"

But in that moment, we pull away from the castle property line and onto the highway, and Finn opens the car with such power, I'm thrust back against my seat. Oh, I'm definitely proposing to this car.

"We're out of range of the castle surveillance cameras now," he says with a grin, shifting into a higher gear. The way he drives isn't actually scary, though, even while zooming along a road that hugs a cliff overlooking the sea. It's powerful, it's controlled. I do *not* let myself wonder if this is any indication of what it would be like to sleep with him. Instead, I sit back and enjoy the feeling of being inside the snug car, watching cold-looking gray waves crash against the rocky shore below.

Finn points out a harbor in the distance and tells me about his love of sailing: how his favorite sound in the world occurs the moment you turn off the engine and you hear those first waves lap against the hull of the boat. I tell him about the time I went kayaking with my senior class and flipped the boat the second I stepped in.

"Don't tell me you're afraid of kayaks too," he teases.

"Flip me once, shame on you," I say defensively. "Flip me twice . . ."

"I'd flip you as many times as you asked," he says suggestively. I ignore him.

He slows the car as we pass a sign that says: Musselburgh, The Honest Town. I point to it. "What's with the motto?"

"Ah, yes. Sweet, isn't it? In the early fourteenth century, after the Earl of Moray died, his successor, the Earl of Mar, tried to bribe the townspeople here in exchange for their loyalty," Finn explains as I nearly press my face to the window, drinking in the charm of the tiny stone houses, some of which look unchanged from the fourteenth century. "The townspeople refused, saying it was their duty to be loyal. The Earl of Mar was impressed by this and called them 'honest men.'"

"I would've taken the money."

"Which is why I told you I'm paying tonight. If I can't win over your friendship with my charm, I'm going to bribe you for it." He deftly parks the car on a narrow side street and says, "I hope you're hungry."

I get out of the car, and we walk toward an area lined with shops and cafés. I look around. "Aren't you worried about getting photographed?" I keep the second part of my question to myself: *Should* I *worry about getting photographed?*

"Not here. There are a few places that have an understanding with the crown."

Finn leads me into a cozy tavern charmingly committed to a nautical theme. One wall is all windows, offering views of the beach. Despite the cloudy evening, there are toddlers running in and out of the surf while nervous parents grab their little hands.

"Can't stay away, can ye?" a mustachioed older man asks as we approach.

"Never, Captain," confirms Finn. "How was Isla's first year of uni? Did she do okay?"

"Better than okay," the man says proudly. He stage-whispers, "She takes after her mum, thank the lord."

Finn chuckles, then gestures at me. "This is my friend, Hannah. Poor thing is from America and needs a meal she won't forget."

"Hello, Hannah," the man says, shaking my hand. He grabs two menus and leads us to a table near a big bay window.

The more time I spend with Finn, the less I can match the sweet guy who asks about a restaurant worker's daughter and who helped me conquer my fear of horses with the playboy from the tabloids. *But isn't that what players do?* a small voice in the back of my mind points out. *They get away with bad behavior* because *they're charming.*

I shake off the cognitive dissonance this devil of a prince is causing me and look over the menu. "What's your go-to meal here?"

"I start with the lobster roll and chips. The lobster? She's succulent. She's fresh. She's—"

"Gendered for some reason."

He gives me a cheeky glare before continuing. "The chips are crispy on the outside, but like clouds on the inside with just the right amount of salt."

"Are you turning yourself on right now?"

"Am I turning *you* on?"

"I swear, if you tell me dessert is in your pants, I'm walking out of here and hitchhiking back to the castle."

He laughs. "Dessert is sticky toffee pudding."

"I don't know what it is, but I'm in."

Captain comes back and takes our order. When Finn says we're both taking his usual, Captain rests a hand on Finn's shoulder. "It's nice to see you with some company finally."

The comment catches me off guard. I assumed when Finn brought me here that I was one in a string of girls. After all, the tabloid photos painted a picture of him that was hard to ignore.

"I didn't take you for the solo-dining type," I say after Captain steps away.

Finn shrugs. "Inveresk Castle has been in my family for generations, and the locals are accustomed to having us around. Me, especially. There aren't many places where I can have a quiet meal on my own, so I come here fairly often."

It's true. There are plenty of other customers in here, all of whom look like very chill retirees, none of whom are so much as looking at Finn.

"What about your family? Do they ever come with you?"

Instead of answering, Finn looks out the window, where the wind is picking up. The families who were playing on the beach are packing up their gear; parents are cleaning off little toddler hands. "Not recently. We're not on the best terms at the moment." A million questions race toward the tip of my tongue, but I bite them back and wait for him to continue. "As I said, they're all in France without me. My parents thought it'd be 'good' for me to have a 'quiet summer' away from distractions. I . . . Um. Well, I recently suffered a minor heartbreak. That's what led to all the partying, which in turn led to becoming 'an embarrassment to us all,' to quote my father." He swallows, as though he can stop the heartbreak from rising up again.

"That's awful. To abandon you like that when you're suffering."

Finn lets out a bitter laugh. "Yes, well, we're not exactly the type of family that gathers round the kitchen table for tea and cozy chats about our feelings."

"Mine either. At least, not my feelings. There never seems to be enough time for those." I pause, then ask gently, "Who was she?"

I can almost hear the gears in Finn's head turning as he tries to decide how much to reveal. "A long-time family friend," he says finally. "She's called Beatrice."

"Sounds complicated," I say, trying to keep my tone neutral.

"A bit, perhaps. There's always been this sort of . . . understanding in my family. That I can date whomever I like, get all the 'unsuitable' girls out of my system, and then eventually settle down with the right kind."

"Like Beatrice?"

"My parents never hid the fact that she was their first choice. Our parents are close. Our *grandparents* are close. So naturally we wanted nothing to do with each other when we were growing up. But last summer, that . . . changed. Beatrice and I kissed for the first time, and this person whom I'd been expected to marry became the person I could actually *see* myself marrying. Our casual friendship turned into a friendship with rather fun benefits, and that turned into something akin to love. At least it did for me."

An ache spreads in my chest for Finn because I know what he's experiencing right now. I know it firsthand. "What happened?"

"We were together for six months. I sincerely thought that was it for me. I thought she was the person I would be with forever. Remember, we hadn't just had six months as a couple, we'd had a lifetime as family friends as well." He shakes his head. "Then, out of nowhere, she pulls the rug out from under me, so to speak, and ends things."

"Why?" I ask, perplexed. Sure, Finn can be a brat, but he's still funny and smart—and too hot for his own good. Never mind that he's a prince, for crying out loud.

"Ah, there's the rub. I have no idea."

"And you dealt with the heartbreak, the lack of closure, by running around looking for distractions that got you in the tabloids," I say, recalling some of the headlines from earlier this year. "Bye-Bye Beatrice: Finn Is a Free Man" and "Prince Says Bea Gone."

"Much to my parents' great delight," Finn adds.

Just then, Captain appears with our lobster rolls and fries—or, rather, *chips.* I take what I mean to be a quick, discreet bite so I don't derail the first sincere conversation Finn and I have ever had, but to my horror, a mortifying moan escapes my lips as I swallow.

"Would you and the lobster roll like some privacy?" Finn asks.

"We might," I say, then take another bite. "God, that's good. This is my first time having lobster."

"You're joking."

I shoot him a look. "We're not all royalty, Mr. I've Spent My Whole Life in Castles."

"Lobster was considered peasant food for most of history, actually. Its association with luxury is quite recent, actually. And besides, doesn't your country have some appalling chain called Red Lobster?"

"I'm tuning you out. Nothing is going to come between me and the lobster. I want to make out with it. I thought I wanted to marry the car we drove here. Now I think I want to marry this sandwich."

"It's probably legal here. Scotland is quite progressive."

I resist the urge to keep the banter going, even though it's much more familiar, comfortable ground for us. "I'm sorry about Beatrice," I say. "Breakups are the worst, even without the entire country reading about it."

"Yes, well . . ." He looks away and bites into a chip.

Perhaps I've made a misstep, acknowledging what I saw online. As penance for my insensitivity, I decide to admit something too.

"I left Wisconsin because my best friend and my boyfriend slept together," I say in a rush because I'm afraid if I say it slowly, I'll cry, and I've already shed too many tears over those two. "Multiple times."

Finn lowers the chip. "Fuck. Really?"

I nod.

"That's awful," he says, shaking his head. "Do you want me to send the royal guard to rough them up?"

"Possibly. Can I think about it and let you know?"

"Certainly. So what happened? I'm all ears and fully prepared to hate them both until I die."

"Dean and I were together for our last two years of high school," I explain, thinking back to how it felt to wear his jacket around my shoulders when I was cold in class, how we'd make out in the back seat of his truck while listening to a playlist I made for him. "Gigi and I had been best friends since kindergarten. I never, in a million years, thought either one of them would betray me. But it turned out, they both did. And had been doing just that for the entirety of our senior year."

"Okay, the royal guard isn't going to be enough for these two," Finn says, frowning. "I'll call the British Army."

"Yeah." My chin trembles. I breathe in and out, determined not to cry.

"How did you find out?" Finn asks, reaching for my hand. "If you don't want to talk about it, you don't—"

"No, it's okay," I say. "On our last day of school, our teachers let us do whatever we wanted. We normally weren't allowed to have phones in class, but at that point, who cared? I was scrolling through my phone, adding different people on Snap that I wanted to keep in contact with, when someone AirDropped me pictures of Gigi and Dean kissing at a party."

"Oh, Hannah . . ." Finn squeezes my hand, sending a surge of warmth up my arm and into my chest, thawing the feelings I tried so hard to lock away.

"I was in shock. I . . . Anyway, after school, I showed them the pictures, they broke down and told me everything. I felt like such an idiot." A tear slips down my cheek.

"Forget the royal guard and the British Army, I might just take care of them myself," Finn says.

He sounds so genuinely angry, I can't help but laugh. I let go of his hand to wipe my eyes and say, "That wouldn't be a *great* way to stay out of the papers."

Captain arrives with our dessert, the famous sticky toffee pudding. "Brilliant," Finn says. "I'm a big believer in eating one's feelings."

The "pudding" looks more like a cake with caramel sauce drizzled on top, and I'm suddenly very into this plan. "Ladies first," Finn says.

The pudding is both dense and moist, and the drizzle

has a sweetness that dances across my tongue. I roll my head back. "This is heaven. I'm in heaven."

"The first bite never gets old," Finn agrees.

People are starting to stare, and I don't think it's because there's a royal in their midst. I don't care. Because to my surprise, I feel more relaxed and comfortable than I have in a very long time.

I sit up. "Finn?"

"Hannah?"

"I'm sorry if I was hard on you. I'm sorry that I misjudged you."

He cocks his head and surveys me, as if waiting for the punch line. "You're serious," he says.

"I'd never lie in the presence of sticky toffee pudding, the holiest of desserts."

"I'd better remember that. Could come in handy someday. And I'm sorry I gave you a reason to see me as a rapscallion." He pauses. "Please, please don't respond with some quote from *Pride and Prejudice* about first impressions."

"Why not? What do you have against Jane Austen?"

"I have nothing but fondness and respect for Ms. Austen. I just don't want you ruining our lovely moment with your appalling accent."

Our lovely moment.

This feels like a fresh start between us. One I'm ready for.

11

I always assumed the muses would sneak up on me. Tap me on the shoulder or whisper in my ear. I wasn't expecting them to knock me upside the head while I'm frantically googling Beatrice's name on my day off.

It's early in the morning, but I barely slept last night. My evening in Musselburgh with Finn left me jittery and with more unanswered questions than I went in with. Namely: What is Beatrice's deal and is she funnier and prettier than I am?

I've been doing research to answer these pressing questions for hours. Seeing how tall and lithe she is, how elegantly she moves through the world, is pure torture. And yet I can't stop. Can't stop until the muses finally shake me from my newfound addiction. I'm equal parts annoyed and excited as I abandon my Beatrice-centric searches to write an idea in the notebook I keep by my bed: *Chocolat meets*

Jane Eyre—a woman learns to heal a Scottish town, and her own family trauma, through food.

I stare at the elevator pitch and then look back to my phone, which is stuck on a news video of Beatrice posing for pictures wearing a dress that probably costs more than my college tuition. In it, she's holding Finn's arm in a way that makes me want to punch her in the jugular.

Okay.

Okay.

It's my day off. During this leisure time, I can continue to internet-stalk a woman I should absolutely not care about, or I can turn my attention to the book idea that just came to me.

The second option is the better one, even though it's intimidating as hell. I've written short stories and poems, but this will be my first attempt at a full novel. Knowing I'll need to aim for eighty thousand words because of the genre has me chewing on my bottom lip. I don't know if I've written that many words in my entire high school career.

But this is what I want. This is what my summer is for. To gain traction for my writing career.

Yes. This distraction is good. This distraction is still making me feel bad about myself, but at least the book is something I can do something about. At least it's progress instead of the mere self-flagellation of staring at images of Beatrice.

I set my phone aside and open to a fresh page in my

notebook. I begin outlining plot points, making character sketches. The more I write down, the more new ideas come to me. My only hang-up so far is that food is at the heart of this story and, as much as I love to eat, I can't really cook.

The ding of a new notification from WhatsApp (the group is currently gossiping about which pop star is rumored to be vacationing nearby) reminds me that I know someone who knows food. A renewed sense of excitement and purpose rushes through me. I make my bed and brush my teeth. I throw on a pair of jeans, a T-shirt, and a cardigan, since it's still early and there's likely a bite in the air. Then I lock up my cottage and start walking toward the castle.

The fact that I can casually walk into a castle on my day off work is hilarious. Gigi can have Dean and his clumsy make-out skills, for all I care. I've got a castle and a bunch of new friends. *Including a royal one,* a voice reminds me. But the term "friend" doesn't feel quite right for what Finn and I are to each other. Not after our evening in Musselburgh.

The fierce protectiveness that came out when I told him about Gigi and Dean, the vulnerability he showed when talking about Beatrice, the way he and I can push each other's buttons as easily as we can make each other laugh . . .

Nope. Absolutely not. I came to Scotland for the good of my career, not to fall for a prince who's probably not even allowed to date an American anyway. After last night, I'm less inclined to believe Finn would sleep with me and toss me out of the castle on my ass. Nonetheless, I will not be a Margaret MacIntyre and push aside my goals to chase a guy.

And I will 100 percent stop googling his ex-girlfriend.

The dew on the grass as I walk to the castle chills my sandal-clad feet, but the sun is out and so are the muses. I continue to daydream about characters and settings until I get to the door I now know leads directly to the kitchen. I knock and then let myself in.

"Ah, Hannah," Ethel greets me. She has a wooden spoon in her hand. I'm worried I might be interrupting something, but the kitchen is spotless, and nothing seems to be on the go. She asks, "Can I make you a full Scottish breakfast?"

"Um . . ." I appreciate the offer. However, there is a good chance I'll end up with black pudding on my plate and I am not prepared to try that yet. Maybe ever.

"Or maybe some drop scones?" she suggests.

I don't know what those are, but they sound safe. "That sounds wonderful, thanks. I'm hoping I can pick your brain about cooking for a book I'm writing."

"Ah, you're a writer, are you?" Ethel begins making batter. "That's just lovely, dear. Ask away."

When she says she doesn't mind if I record the conversation, I pull out my phone and set it on the counter between us. Ethel cooks while I pepper her with questions about her life and her relationship with her job.

"I was raised in a house with six kids," she says, measuring out ingredients she then whisks together with a lot of might despite her advanced age. Something tells me she's freakishly strong and could probably beat me at arm wrestling. "Eldest girl, I was, so I was an extra mum to all the littles. I learned that the best way to get them to behave was to bribe them with sweets. We didn't have the money to buy such extravagances, so I learned to make them all myself. Course, then mum didn't want to do any cooking when she discovered what I could do. Cooking for royals is much easier, much less pressure than cooking for five hungry siblings, that's for sure."

She ladles the batter onto a griddle, and I stop the recording for now. As it turns out, drop scones are essentially pancakes. She sets us both up at the island with the barstools where Finn and I had stew the other day. Between the place settings, she adds various jams as well as a jar of Nutella.

As we eat, we discuss different foods and how meals can impact moods and show affection.

"I don't make these drop scones for anyone," Ethel tells me. "But I've taken a shine to you. And I don't seem to be the only one."

"What do you mean?" I ask, assuming she's referring to Caro or maybe Beverly.

"Don't be coy, you know who I'm referring to." She puts more jam on her drop scones and points at me with her fork. "You should know how nice it is to see Finn smiling again. That lad, walking around here, just crabbit at the world. Or out carousing and making a mess of things for their highnesses. You've had a nice effect on him."

I look down at my plate, afraid Ethel will be able to read everything on my face I don't want to acknowledge myself. And then, because I simply can't help myself or my self-flagellation, I ask, "What's Beatrice like?"

I can't stop thinking about whether she made him laugh and why the hell she ended things with him. I'm hoping if Ethel can tell me the truth, I can stop obsessing.

"Oh, she's a fine young lady. Comes from a good family, has nice manners," Ethel tells me, her voice even. Then she quietly adds, "Doesn't seem to have a sense a humor, though. And sure broke the poor lad's heart."

I take an extra-large bite of Nutella and drop scone so Ethel can't see how pleased I am to hear that. *Beatrice isn't funny. She may be perfect in every other way, but she doesn't laugh. She doesn't make* him *laugh.*

Just then, Caro bursts through the door. "Hannah! There you are. I've been looking all over for you."

"Don't you be coming in my kitchen with that kind of chaos, Caro," Ethel warns her. "You know the rules. You knock and then come in."

"Sorry, ma'am, but this is an emergency," Caro says, still frantic. "Our sketch troupe might have a place to perform for Edinburgh Fringe! Before they give us the spot, they want us to do a show there to see if we'll draw a crowd or be funny or all of the above and so in order to do that, they want us to perform there tomorrow and I need you to come and I need everyone to come and laugh a lot and be really lovely so we can make our dreams come true."

Between Caro's accent and the speed at which she just delivered the speech, it takes me a minute to process what she just said. As soon as I do, I run up and hug her. "Of course I'll come. I'm so excited for you."

"I'll come too," Ethel says behind us, "not that you invited me."

"Please come, Ethel. You know I want you and Beverly to be there," Caro says, her hands in a prayer. Then she hugs me again, squeals, says, "Okay, thank you, I have to go and rehearse with Leah and Duffie," and runs off.

I'm so happy for Caro, I'm light on my feet as I help Ethel clear our plates. A new message lights up my phone, which is still on the counter. It's from Finn.

> Rosie told me she misses you. How about another riding lesson tonight after supper?

Ethel doesn't even try to hide the fact that she's looking over my shoulder at the screen, reading every word.

"Riding lesson, my erse," she mumbles.

Still keen on keeping my name out of the gossip circles, I try to explain the text. "I'm scared of horses and Finn's helping me conquer my fear." Ethel's responding look of disbelief makes me blush. I whisper, "We're just friends anyway."

"Friendship, my erse," Ethel says.

I ignore her and text Finn.

I don't have Rosie's number. Can you tell her I'd love to?

I shiver despite the heat of the kitchen. *We're just friends,* I tell myself. Even if I *was* accidentally developing feelings for him, nothing about the two of us makes sense, starting with the fact that I am Beatrice's opposite in every superficial *and* meaningful way. Finn should be with a Beatrice, not an American who openly mocks the monarchy. As though reading my thoughts, Ethel stops me before I go.

"I'm glad you came in," she says. "You seem to fit in here at the castle. We're happy to have you."

It's a simple statement, one that shouldn't form a lump in my throat and give rise to hope. And yet, it does. For the first time in a long time, I feel as though I belong.

12

Finn doesn't notice me right away when I enter the stable, giving me the opportunity to watch him nuzzle a beautiful dark horse who's *way* too big for my liking. I still can't reconcile the Finn I've gotten to know over the past few days with the one I've read about. Maybe it's my non-monarchist upbringing, but I can't seem to think of him as royalty—he just seems like a normal boy with a secretly soft heart and a wicked sense of humor.

Finn gives the horse a kiss on the nose and feeds him something from his hand. I clear my throat. Finn hears me and turns around. His face lights up when he sees me, his mouth breaking into a grin. "I'll go fetch Rosie," he says, leading her out of the stall and into the crossties. Her soulful eyes are telling me not to be afraid. Not of her, not of Finn. "She's already groomed, so I just need to tack her up."

I pet her neck and breathe in her outdoorsy scent. "Can you teach me how to do it?" I ask.

Finn walks me through the steps of positioning the pad and the saddle and buckling the girth. Then he shows me how to put on her bridle, something I'm definitely not ready to do myself as it involves putting your fingers in the horse's mouth to get them to accept the bit.

He hands me Rosie's reins, then goes to grab his own horse, the dark brown one. "This is Ivanhoe," he says. "Don't be jealous, Hannah, but Ivanhoe is my one true love."

"I'm not jealous," I say too quickly, too sincerely, which makes Finn laugh.

We lead the horses out of the stable where, once again, Finn helps me into the saddle from the mounting block. Although this time, he offers a comically wide berth, like he thinks I'll electrocute him if we touch. He reminds me how to hold the reins, then mounts his own horse, eschewing the steps entirely. Instead, he places one foot in the stirrup, then hoists himself up in one smooth motion.

"Show-off," I say.

He clucks to Ivanhoe, who takes off at a brisk walk. I'm just about to squeeze Rosie with my calves, like Finn showed me, but she follows Ivanhoe without being asked. "Good girl," I whisper. "Thank you."

Ivanhoe begins to prance in place and toss his head. It's clear he wants to speed up. Finn remains tall and relaxed in the saddle, seemingly unbothered by the fact that his enormous horse seems poised to take off at any moment. "Relax, mate," he says, reaching down to pat Ivanhoe's neck.

Ivanhoe settles down as we walk down the drive and turn onto the dirt path Finn and I went down before, the one that cut through the meadow. "Want to try a trot?" Finn asks.

"I'm not sure. How fast is that?"

"It's a jog. And you'll be fine. Rosie will take care of you. Besides, you have a natural seat."

"*Excuse* me?"

"Get your mind out of the gutter, you dirty American. It means you're naturally balanced in the saddle." He gives Ivanhoe an invisible signal and the horse springs forward. Rosie follows suit and breaks into a quick, slightly bouncy jog.

"Oh god," I say, grabbing on to the front of the saddle for balance as my teeth rattle in my head.

"Try posting," Finn calls over his shoulder. "Like this." I watch him rise up and down in time to Ivanhoe's steps.

I try to mimic him but the movement is awkward, and frankly, I'm terrified of letting go of the saddle. But then I take a deep breath, press down on the stirrups, hover for a moment, then lower myself back down.

"There you go," Finn says. "Just like that."

I bounce around for another minute, and then suddenly feel myself begin to move in a rhythm. Up down, up down, up down, all in time with Rosie's steps. "I'm doing it!"

"That you are, cowgirl. Well done."

We're still going a little faster than I'd like, but it feels more thrilling than terrifying. The path narrows as we approach the woods up ahead, but Rosie's pace remains steady. I take another deep breath, and sigh as the scent of pine floods my senses.

I'm happier than I've been in a really long time. Maybe ever. I try to capture every image, squeezing it as I'm experiencing it now and as a memory.

"You okay to keep going?" Finn calls over his shoulder.

"Yes!"

And then suddenly, we're in the woods, Rosie trotting briskly behind Ivanhoe. It's like something out of a movie. Out of a fairy tale. The path is so narrow, tree branches form a canopy above us, giving the dappled light a greenish tint. We round a bend and suddenly we're riding alongside a brook, crystal clear water surging around moss-covered rocks.

Finn slows his horse to a walk, and Rosie follows suit. "Shall we take a break?" Finn asks. He dismounts gracefully, then comes over to help me slide off, much less gracefully. We lead the horses to a quieter section of the brook to let them drink, then Finn hooks their reins over a branch and motions for me to follow him to a patch of grass overlooking the water.

I stretch to accommodate the growing ache of muscles I didn't know I have.

"Okay, so riding actually is a workout, then," I say,

reaching my hands to the sky. My shirt shimmies up with the motion. I can feel the cool air on my stomach—and I catch Finn looking.

"Try to control yourself," I tease him.

He tears his eyes away from me and nods toward the lake. "Beautiful evening for a swim," he says.

I can't deny that it is. The sun is setting slowly; the air is the temperature of fun and bad decisions.

"You're just trying to get me to go skinny-dipping with you," I say.

"I'm truly not," he protests. "I'll prove it." He takes off his shoes and socks and runs into the water with the rest of his clothes still on until it's deep enough to dive under. When he emerges, his hair is slicked back and appears darker, giving me an unobstructed view of his handsome-as-a-devil face. But that's not even the best part. Because the only things more chiseled than Prince Finneas's jawline are his chest and stomach, both of which I can see clearly, thanks to the shirt clinging to him like a second skin.

"Hot damn," I whisper.

"What was that?" he calls back. I shake my head to indicate I didn't say anything—at least not anything meant for his ears. He waves me over, the water rippling around him as he moves. "Don't be a fraidy-cat, American Hannah. Come on, then."

In a rare moment, I don't allow myself to think. I take off my sneakers and socks and run in, splashing without grace, without a care in the world. My shorts and cropped shirt immediately flood with water and stick to me. But, oh, the water feels incredible. Just cool enough to counteract the humidity I've been fighting all day. When my toes can no longer feel the squishy bottom of the lake, I frog-kick my legs and swim until I reach Finn. Unable to touch, I start treading. We're facing each other, grinning like two fools who don't care how uncomfortable the ride back up to the stables will be. Ethel's words ring in my ears.

Friendship, my erse.

"The last time I treaded water this long, it was to pass my swimming test," I tell him. "I think I was twelve."

"Poor teeny tiny little Hannah," he says. He cups one hand and squeezes his fist so that water squirts toward my face.

"Hey," I protest, and reach for his offending hand. He squirts me with the other one and I'm simultaneously attempting to stop him while trying not to drown. But I don't struggle for long because he reaches an arm around my waist to hold me, steady me. Instead of keeping his fists closed to stop him from spraying me again, my arms end up on his shoulders.

My heart is pounding. No person has ever looked as gorgeous to me as he looks in this lake, in this twilight. All I want—all I'm desperate to do—is to press my lips against his, just to see if they're as soft as they look. My lids are heavy. His are too. Our noses are about to touch.

Suddenly, he pulls away. It's so jarring, so humiliating, I forget to tread water and my shoulders submerge. His hands reach for my waist to lift me, but I've caught myself.

"We should head back before it gets dark," he says in a tone I can't read, a tone I don't like.

"Yeah. Definitely," I say, and swim toward shore without looking back.

13

The journey to Edinburgh the next day is comprised of what could be described as a motorcade of clown cars. I ride, squished in a back seat between Ethel and Beverly. They talk over me while two elderly tour guides, Edgar and Simon, talk over each other in the front. I catch snippets of gossip about tourists from the front seat and snippets of gossip about my coworkers in the back seat. I'd love every second of it if I wasn't still so in my head about what happened at the lake.

This is Caro's big event, and I want to be able to cheer her on with my whole chest, but it's aching. I want to avoid Finn for the rest of my life and forget he exists. It's pretty hard when I work and live at his house and am surrounded, daily, by merchandise with his face on it.

The pub that Caro, Leah, and Duffie will be performing at gave them a four-thirty p.m. performance slot, which is too early for the evening crowd and too late for the lunch crowd. It feels a little like the pub is setting them up to fail, but the pub owner clearly has no idea how beloved Caro and Leah are at Inveresk. As for the third member of their trio, Duffie seems to be tolerated. According to my drive here, the castle gossip mill has been churning about him and Caro for a while now—and they're all Team Caro.

Despite the awkward start time, dozens of castle staff are squished into the venue.

"Greetings and salutations," Duffie says from a small stage that's set up for tonight's pub quiz. We politely clap.

Caro steps forward with outstretched arms. "Thank you to the World's End for having us. We are—"

"Perimenopausal and Knackered," Leah says, sitting on a stool behind her two costars.

Duffie and Caro look embarrassed. They turn around and the three of them have a whisper-fight. The only thing we as an audience can make out is quips of "We decided on a name," and "*You* decided on a name," and Leah insisting, "I was just being honest." It ends with Leah relenting and whispering, "Fine. Let's do this properly, I promise not to interrupt."

"Good early evening," Leah says, walking to the front of the stage. "Apologies for the delay. Thank you so much for coming."

We break into wild applause.

"We'll be doing some comedy sketches for you that we hope you enjoy," Caro says. She looks amazing on stage—bright-eyed, excited. "And now to properly introduce ourselves. We! Are!"

"*Perimenopausal and Knackered!*" Duffie declares, catching us all off guard and earning them their first of many genuine laughs from all of us. For the rest of the show, I'm able to forget and simply enjoy.

We pile back into our clown cars afterward. Instead of going home, we head to a second location where I learn two very important things. One: Friday night is karaoke night at a hole-in-the-wall bar called Look Sharp! (yes, with the exclamation point) in the tiny town of Inveresk. Most of the staff from the castle are religious attendees of this weekly tradition. The second thing I learn—and quickly—is that of those religious attendees, less than half can carry a tune. Bless their enthusiastic hearts, the lack of natural musicality doesn't stop any of them from earnestly belting their favorite tunes.

I'm having the best time listening to Edgar, the tour guide, sing Rod Stewart's classic "Do Ya Think I'm Sexy?" followed by a housekeeper named Adelaide who warbles her way through Annie Lennox's "Walking on Broken Glass." I hoot and applaud and yell with the rest of my colleagues, laughing until my cheeks hurt.

"Come on, Hannah," Caro begs. "Sing a duet with me. It'll be a riot."

"I'd much rather remain a supportive member of the audience, thanks," I tell her, nursing my pint. This is the best and only true distraction I've experienced since I utterly humiliated myself in the woods with Finn yesterday. There's no way he'll ever talk to me again. After all the times I rebuffed his flirty comments, I've been the one who's tried to kiss him. Twice. Yes, in both moments, I was certain that he wanted it as much as I did, but upon reflection, how could that possibly be true? I must have misinterpreted his signs, the way he helped me down from Rosie or tried to make sure I didn't drown in a lake. I might as well be the court jester of Inveresk Castle.

Just thinking about it makes me turn red—I can feel the hot blush of embarrassment claim my face in the middle of Look Sharp! and take a huge gulp of my beer.

"Oh! I found us a song!" Caro says, taking my beer from me and putting it down on the table. She points at one of the songs in the binder she's been flipping through. But I can't pay attention because there's been a shift in the crowd. My coworkers are all sitting up a little straighter, self-consciously taking small sips from their drinks instead of downing them the way they were moments ago. People have stopped what they're doing to whisper to one another, and they're all staring at the entrance.

A new group has entered the bar, and their appearance has obliterated any chance I had at not humiliating myself tonight.

No no no no no no no.

I want to crawl under the table. I want to run out the back door. I want to become a magician and disappear in a puff of smoke.

"Is that a yes? You'll sing this one with me?" Evidently, Caro hasn't noticed the vibes change because she's still pointing excitedly at the binder. I don't even look to see what it is. I just know I can't be sitting here when the only available table is right next to ours. I've got to get away from here, even if that means getting on the stage. Finn can't talk to me if I'm singing, so that's exactly what I'm going to do.

"Sure, looks great," I tell her, following her to the karaoke host's stand. She tells the host which song we're singing, and we queue up, waiting for Annie Lennox to stop walking on broken glass.

I refuse to look at Finn and his friends. I'm carefree! I'm buzzed on half a beer! I'm having the time of my life! No one needs to feel sorry for me!

The song ends and Caro and I take the stage, much to great applause. I know it's mostly for Caro, who's deservedly well loved among our coworkers. We each park ourselves in front of a microphone as the opening notes to "Under Pressure" begin.

"I get to be David Bowie," she declares to me via the microphone.

Perfect. Not only am I suddenly singing karaoke in front

of all my coworkers and the guy who has rejected me not once, but twice, but I have to take the part sung by Freddie Mercury. No problem. It's not like he was known for his operatic vocal gymnastics or anything.

"I need my beer," I say a little too loudly into the microphone over the song's introduction. Within seconds, Leah's handing me my beer and I'm chugging it as the bar cheers me on. I miss Freddie's opening "oom-ba-bah" or whatever he says there, but finish drinking just in time to sing "*Pressure!*" with Caro.

Caro's naturally unabashed and therefore a killer karaoke performer. I've got liquid courage and a screw-it-I've-already-lived-my-worst-case-scenario-in-front-of-Finn attitude and so I give myself over to embodying Freddie Mercury's performance, despite being only a passable singer. By the second chorus, the whole bar, patrons and staff alike, are singing along with us. Caro and I do kicks and throw our hands up in the air. The song ends and we receive the night's first standing ovation.

I spare a glance at Finn's table, which I've managed to avoid looking at for roughly four minutes. He and his friends are on their feet, whistling and hollering. I give a cheeky little curtsy while avoiding any eye contact with him. When the cheering dies down, Caro and I hold hands and walk back to our table. I choose the chair that puts my back toward Finn.

We've just sat down when Duffie, blond hair a mess,

races over. He pulls Caro up, wraps his arms around her, and spins her. The crowd falls silent as we wait to see what's to come.

Once the spin is over and Caro's back on her feet, Duffie dips her and kisses her in front of everyone. The bar erupts. Duffie has very publicly declared them an item and Caro looks overjoyed. I whistle and clap along with everyone else. Duffie takes the extra seat at our table, which is expected and wonderful, however, he also takes Caro's full attention, leaving me stranded. The fact that there's no longer a queue waiting to sing (evidently no one wants to follow our karaoke performance or that movie-style kiss) doesn't help.

"American Hannah, hi! That performance was brilliant," Bethany says from behind me.

I turn around in my chair and force a smile. "Oh, thank you. I couldn't have done it without the peer pressure of my costar and the liquid courage of my beer."

"You're my shero," Mhairi enthuses.

"Come sit with us," Callum says with a wave. "Your tablemates are too busy making googly eyes at each other to notice if you leave. We promise to pay attention to you."

The three of them are so sweet and I genuinely would love to hang out with them, but there's the guy who rejected me right beside them. Not that I'm looking at him. Finn could be doing jumping jacks for all I know.

I can't avoid him forever because Caro and Duffie are

now fully making out at our table. Reluctantly, I move to the only unoccupied chair. It just happens to be beside the guy I won't acknowledge.

"Nice to see you three again," I say to Callum, Mhairi, and Bethany.

"Same. I think I love you," Callum replies. "Maybe it's too soon to say, I don't care. When someone walks into your life and does Freddie proud, you can't ignore that."

"I'm flattered," I tell him with a laugh.

Beside me, Finn is silent. Callum, Bethany, and Mhairi ask about working the gift shop, which means Finn's filled them in at least a little. I wonder what else they know. So far there are no looks of pity. That's a good sign.

"Tell us," Mhairi says, leaning on the table. "Do people come in and take the mickey out of Finneas's ugly mug on all the mugs?"

"No, but I do," I reply, which garners a laugh.

"Do you do fake accents just to keep yourself entertained?" Callum asks.

"I don't. In fact, my boss has informed me to never do a Scottish accent again," I say, sparing my first glance at Finn. His eyes are fixed on me with an intensity that makes me look away. "But I think I just need some practice."

"I'm not technically your boss," Finn says low enough so that the others can't hear. I ignore him.

"Oi," Mhairi says to Caro and Duffie, breaking them apart. "Pass us the binder? I'm feeling a song come on."

Finn excuses himself to go to the bar. With his back to me, I'm free to watch him, to admire how he moves easily through the crowd, the kindness and attention he gives everyone he passes. He exudes warmth in a way that wraps me up and makes me break. I look down at the table, wishing I had another drink or something to do with my hands. Sitting here, being so close to him, is making me antsy in a way I can't take.

When Finn reaches the bar, he leans over to talk to the bartender, who then gestures at the emcee.

The emcee turns on his microphone and announces, "His highness has just covered everyone's tab for tonight and would like to buy the next round as well."

Everyone cheers, but no one seems surprised. This is just who Finn is. A guy with a great big heart. A guy whose darkest time was showcased to the world to pick apart like magpies on roadkill and yet not only did he get through it, but he didn't let it change his best instincts.

I like him so much I think I'm going to cry.

"I'm going to get some air," I say to his friends, who are still poring over the karaoke song binder.

I weave my way through the bar to an outdoor porch where people go to smoke and vape. Thankfully there's no one out there. It's just me and the alley cats. I lean my elbows on the railing and look up at the night sky. Wispy clouds pass by the moon, shifting the light and shadows.

The door opens and shuts behind me, but I don't look to see who's here. I don't feel like talking to anyone.

"Have you considered dual careers in writing and performing?" Finn says.

I still don't turn around. I can't. I'm certain every feeling I have for him is written on my face and I won't let him see it. Getting rejected a third time is a shame I really can't bear right now.

"Hey," he says softer, gentler. His hand rests on my arm. I have to resist leaning into the warmth of him.

"You're not going to sing? You know the people would love it," I say. My voice sounds strange, even to my own ears. I watch a cat across the alleyway rub itself against a building and seemingly pounce on nothing. *I can relate, buddy. I've been pouncing on nothing since I got to Scotland.*

"No one wants to hear me sing," Finn says. "Despite years of vocal lessons when I was young, I'm unable to carry even the lightest of tunes. My elder sister, Amelia, is quite the soprano. She barred me from singing years ago."

Amelia's photo came up during my Google searches of Finn. She's the very essence of an English-rose beauty. I try to think of a retort, and nothing comes to mind. I try to think of anything, but my thoughts and feelings are so big and jumbled. . . .

"American Hannah?" he says. "Why won't you look at me?"

"I'll look at you," I say, and absolutely do *not* look at him.

He sighs and leans against the railing next to me. "This is the most guarded you've ever been with me. Even that first night at the pub was better than this."

What do you expect? I want to say. *I'm humiliated.* Instead, I say, "Shouldn't you get back inside? Your friends are probably wondering where you are."

He's quiet. The pull I feel to him is unbearable—made worse knowing it's unrequited. That somehow, I've conjured this chemistry on my own and it's completely one-sided.

"I'm such an idiot," I accidentally say out loud. I don't even care anymore. I swore to myself I wouldn't fall for him, believing I was too smart.

"You're not," he says. "But I am a total and complete fuckup."

That gets my attention. Finally, I look at him. "What do you mean?"

Now that I can see his deep hazel eyes, the slope of his nose, the way the moonlight hits his copper hair, my knees go weak. I turn my attention back to the cat.

"In the woods." His voice is low.

"I—" I'm about to make an excuse, claim I was just joking there in the water, playing him, but he cuts me off.

"No, it's my turn to speak." His sigh is layered. Regretful. "I wanted so badly to kiss you, Hannah."

"Then why didn't you?" My heart rises into my throat.

"Because I was scared, because I swore to myself that I wouldn't get tangled up in anything real, not after what happened with Beatrice. Because you are so precious and funny and clever. Because the way I feel about you makes me nervous."

My breathing becomes shallow. "I make you nervous?"

He chuckles lightly. "Do you know what my friends said tonight?"

"What?" I stop watching the alley cat. I steel myself to look at him without melting. It's not possible. Not when I know who he is on the inside in addition to who he is on the outside.

"They told me I'm an utter knob if I don't push my fears aside and take the leap." He pauses. "Hannah?"

"Finn?" I reply, unable to wrap my head around what he's just said. He wanted to pursue me. He wants to take the leap with me. My arms are ready to reach out and grab him. At the same time, my heart and my pride warn me to be careful.

"Can I kiss you?" he asks.

I nod. It's all I can do not to throw myself at him. Instead, I gingerly take a step toward him. He takes a step toward me. I trace down his arms with my fingers, which causes his breathing to hitch. Slowly, so slowly, he brings one hand onto the small of my back and cups my jaw with the other. I lean into his touch and bring my hands up his firm stomach, his chest. My fingers graze the collar of his shirt as they wrap around his neck. He shivers in response.

The air between us is so charged and heady and we haven't even kissed yet. There's a tremor in my hand, so I steady myself against him. We lean into each other farther, holding each other, holding each other up. I'm certain my heart will burst out of my chest at any moment.

And then his head dips. I lift onto my tiptoes in response. Finn's mouth, soft and sweet, finds mine and it's as though I've been starved until this moment. The pressure of this kiss alternates between tentative and deep, full of longing. His arms pull me into him until we're pressed close. Closer. I can no longer tell where he begins and I end. When his tongue sweeps into my mouth, I open wider for him. All I know, all I want to know, is *this.*

Minutes pass or hours or lifetimes of us kissing and holding and expressing everything we've tried to push away since the night we met. It's perfect, it's everything.

And it's interrupted when his phone chimes.

We both freeze. I feel his mouth smile against mine. I laugh into it. It's such an intimate thing. Our foreheads are touching, he's still holding me close, but he reaches one hand into his pocket to retrieve his phone, apologizing as he does.

"I would normally ignore such a rude interruption of such a wonderful thing, but there's a specific chime I'm not supposed to—"

"It's okay," I say, and lower onto my feet. Letting go of him is agony. I do it anyway so he can read his message. My hands are shaking even more now. I wrap my arms around myself.

When he sees the text, his face goes ashen. He swallows. "Hannah, I am so, so sorry, but I . . ." His gaze bounces from the phone to me to the back door and back again. "I have to go."

"It's fine, I get it," I reassure him, still trying to recover from our kiss. Worry creeps up on me. "Is everything okay with you though?"

He doesn't answer; he simply disappears back into the bar.

14

The gift shop has been busier than ever this morning. Tour bus after tour bus is coming through and people are here to spend. I've already run to the back twice to restock our selection of socks. I don't get it, but today's crowd is really into socks.

At least the flurry is keeping me out of my head. I barely slept last night, replaying the kiss with Finn, followed by his face when he received that text. He left so abruptly, and I don't even know why. Eventually, I abandoned the idea of sleeping and used the hours to write the first chapter of my book. Why waste my time overthinking an amazing kiss when I can overthink every single word I write of a new manuscript?

At work, it's particularly difficult keeping Finn off my mind. I'm literally surrounded by his image. Finn in uniform! Finn on horseback! Finn standing stoically between his parents and older siblings, his hand on his younger sister's shoulder! I swear to god the army of Finn bobbleheads is taunting me every time I walk by.

When we finally close up, my body is buzzing and I'm desperate to get outside.

"Hey, Caro, want to go for a walk or something? I've got a bit of cabin fever."

"Aye, that happens to me when the shop is too crowded all day," she says, setting the alarm for the shop's security.

I take a deep breath of fresh air while she locks up. Afraid I'm being too needy, I ask, "Are you busy? Plans with Duffie?"

"Nah, I'd love to cut about." She gives me a mischievous grin. "We could go nick a golf cart from the course."

"There's a golf course here?" It's nuts to think about how much of the grounds I've covered on horseback, and yet I still haven't seen half of it.

"Aye." Caro pockets the keys and slips her arm through mine. "The course is open to the public until five, which means by now all the posh golfers have buggered off and we can go for a tear in the carts."

That sounds exactly like what I need right now. "I'm in."

Excited, we jog through gardens and past the greenhouse until we reach the perfectly maintained golf course. It looks as though each blade of grass has been measured and cut precisely. The greens around us are so vibrant, they almost hurt my eyes. Caro pulls us around to the garage, where staff are hosing down the carts and refilling the tiny golf pencils and scorekeeping pads, the towels, and complimentary water bottles.

"This is Hannah, everyone," Caro says. I say hello back to the chorus of people greeting me. "Can you believe this poor thing has been working with me for days and days and she didn't know about the course?"

"You've *got* to give her a tour," a beefy guy with a bright ginger beard agrees. He leads us over to a spare cart and tells us to have fun. "Just have the cart back in an hour or so, yeah?"

I let Caro drive, since she knows where she's going. We start off along a path, Caro weaving recklessly until I'm laughing and almost falling out of the open side. She takes us to the ninth hole because she says it's her favorite, and I can see why. The view from the tee is spectacular. Ahead of us a forest parts, giving us views of the sun behind rolling pastoral hills.

She cracks open a water bottle and passes it to me before opening one for herself. We sip quietly and take in the beauty of this place.

"So what happened to you last night?" Caro asks.

"What do you mean?" I ask, despite knowing precisely what she means. I'm stalling. I want to tell *someone* about what happened with Finn, and I'd love that to be Caro. But I'm also worried about castle gossip and making things difficult for him. He's in enough trouble with his family already. It occurs to me that someone could've seen us last night. I haven't checked the castle employees' group chat to see if anyone's said anything.

"I mean, you dafty lass," Caro says, furrowing her eyebrows. "You disappeared without saying goodbye."

I hate that I've hurt Caro's feelings when she's been nothing but lovely to me. I hate that I can't confide in her about what really happened last night between me and Finn.

"I'm sorry. But I'm dying to find out what happened between you two after karaoke. Kissing you in front of everyone? That was quite the grand gesture."

Pink-cheeked and bright-eyed, Caro turns back into the bubbly person I've grown to adore as she rests her arm on the back of the seat and pulls a leg up under her. "Can you believe he just laid it on thick in front of everyone? I mean, this is a bloke who's been dancing around our situationship for ages."

I admit, I've been skeptical of Duffie and his fuckboy antics, but last night just might change my mind.

"Tell me what happened afterwards. Spare no detail."

She tells me about how he drove her home and apologized for being too scared to do anything real with her—worried it would ruin their sketch troupe with Leah. But he realized that only doing things halfway was worse, especially since he was in love with her.

"He told you he loves you?" I say with a squeal. She nods, grinning hugely. "I'm so happy for you."

And I am. But I'm also fighting the elation and confusion from my own evening. It must be written all over my face because Caro nudges me with her knee and says, "What about you? Are you going to tell me why you ghosted last night?"

Kissing and telling almost always comes with a bit of danger. That danger is magnified when the kiss involves the symbolic leader of your friend's country. I look up at Caro's open, curious face. I may have lingering issues, thanks to what happened with Dean and Gigi back home, but Caro is genuine. My instincts tell me I can trust her, so I take the risk.

"Finn came outside to find me last night," I begin, watching her eyes widen. "He . . . kissed me."

She claps a hand over her mouth, then removes it and yells, "*I knew it!!* How was the kiss?"

I close my eyes, remembering the way he cupped my jaw and held my body close to his. "Life-alteringly good."

"Oh my days, I knew it, I knew it, I knew it." Caro stands up and points directly at my face. "There are sparks between you, like, *ohmygod* sparks, and I absolutely *knew* you two had it bad."

"You can't tell *anyone*," I warn her. She nods. I pull her back down to sit beside me, relieved to have someone to talk to about this. Holding it in has been psychological torture. "Okay, but then he got a text, got all weird, and took off."

Caro looks as confused as I feel. Slowly, something

dawns on her. "Ohhhh . . . I wager I know what it was about. It's in the email we got from Beverly this morning."

"What email?" I turned off my notifications in case anything came in from Gigi or Dean and I haven't checked my inbox today.

"The one about the castle being closed to the public tomorrow." Caro pulls out her phone to show me and sees the time. "Ach, we've got to head back."

"What's going on?" I say, pulling out my own phone to scan the email. Caro says the words at the same time I'm reading them.

"The royal family. They're coming here."

My stomach flips in a way that has nothing to do with the U-turn Caro has just performed at top speed.

Finn's family will be at the castle. Those ones who expect him to get "unsuitable" girls like me out of his system before he finds his next Beatrice. Some posh girl with three last names, who knows how to waltz *and* gracefully dismount a horse.

This isn't good.

This *really* isn't good.

"Thanks for the spin," Caro says when we get back, parking the cart in front of the beefy ginger.

I think I say "thank you" as well, but my mind is another place. Is Finn going to sneak out to see me? Will he have to be on his best behavior, given everything that went down before his family left for France?

Or will he go the other route and *introduce* me to his family?

I can't decide what'd be worse: being treated like some shameful secret or being forced to interact with the literal king and queen of England.

"Keep up," Caro says as we walk back to the castle. "I don't want to miss it."

"Miss what?"

"Their entrance. I'm not sure if James and Amelia are coming too, or if it's just Penelope. She's got the best style. And she and Finn seem really close. It's adorable."

Caro and I pause as two vintage Rolls-Royces come up the drive. They both have convertible tops, giving full view of the passengers. The first one has King Augustus and Queen Charlotte in it, Princess Penelope between them. I note that Finn's younger sister has his same copper hair and high cheekbones.

I knew, logically, that Finn's parents were the king and queen. I've come across countless images of them since I started working in the gift shop. But seeing them in the flesh feels surreal.

The second car rolls up behind the first, and my heart lurches as I spot Finn. At first, I assume the poised woman beside him must be Amelia, but when I get a closer look, the nervous excitement in my stomach turns to nausea.

There, looking regal and perfect, is Beatrice.

Caro smacks my leg with her hand, reminding me to

curtsy as they drive by. I can't help but raise my lowered head as Finn's car slowly passes. He sees me and looks away, as though he has no idea who I am or what it's like to make me laugh, to kiss me.

What are we to each other now that his family's back? It's the question I asked myself moments ago, and now I have my answer.

Nothing.

Whatever was growing between us is now over.

15

This is the second time someone I've gotten close to, someone I was falling for, has chosen another girl. First Dean, now Finn.

It's me. There's something wrong with *me.* I'm broken or unlovable. Or maybe just annoying? I don't know. All I know is *it's me.* Since I'm dipping into self-destructive thought loops already, I grab my phone. Screw my summer resolution not to look at any of my social media. There's only one way to get the image of Finn looking right through me out of my head. Only one way to stop seeing perfect Beatrice beside him.

I sit down on my bed with my girl dinner of cheese, crackers, and fruit, and reload Instagram and TikTok back onto my phone. Like a little scavenger, I immediately begin poring over everything I've missed. I start out with Dean. So far, he's been on a fishing trip with his guy friends, and he's celebrated his dad's fiftieth birthday. I stare at his familiar dark hair and bright blue eyes and wait for the pain of loss to wash over me. But it never comes. I don't feel anything when I look at him now. Somewhere, between tearfully confronting him about cheating and where I am now, I got over him. But at the moment, I want to pour vinegar in my wounds and looking through Dean's posts isn't doing it, so I move on to Gigi's.

Painstakingly, I go through every single picture and caption she's posted, every TikTok she's made. The first thing I notice is that Dean isn't in any of her content. Not even in the background. There are photos of her with her volleyball friends out for ice cream, selfies of a new hairstyle she's trying out. A few videos of her dog are scattered here and there. Dean is nowhere. I put cheese on a cracker and bite into it angrily. Yes, I'm getting crumbs in my bed, and no, I don't care. Because if Gigi and Dean weren't even going to be together once I was out of the way, what was even the point of them sneaking around for the better part of a year? Was it just for the thrill? If they didn't have real feelings for each other, why couldn't they have chosen someone else to sneak around with? Why do the one thing that would hurt me the most?

I scroll through every post again to see if I missed something. The only thing I seemed to have glazed over is that Gigi looks happy. Really happy. The realization sends a wave of miserable nausea through me so intense that for a moment, I'm sure I'm going to throw up. I push my plate away and put my head between my knees, waiting for the nausea to pass. The betrayal was painful enough. The easy way she's moved on without me is excruciating. She was supposed to visit me in Scotland this summer. We were going to meet up every other weekend once we were in college. After getting our degrees, we planned to get an apartment and decorate it together and, dammit, she was supposed to be my best friend for life, and she threw that all away just so she could screw my boyfriend again and again and again.

I can't be in this cottage anymore. I can't breathe in here. I need to do something that makes me feel free. I need to run or to scream or to . . .

I know exactly what I need to do.

I put on a pair of boots, throw my hair in a ponytail, and walk out the door, leaving my plate and phone on my bed. The speed with which I'm walking makes my muscles stretch and ache; perspiration forms down my back and between my breasts, but I don't slow down. I can't.

I reach the stables. The staff who look after the horses seem to have left for the evening, so I go straight to Rosie's stall. Seeming to sense my arrival, she sticks her neck out and whickers. "Hi, there," I say, scratching her behind the ears. "What do you say, girl? Feel like going for a ride?"

Then I hesitate. Saying the words aloud makes it clear how foolish I'm being. I have no idea what I'm doing. I could get hurt. I could get *fired*. I don't think a summer job in the gift shop entitles you to the royal family's horses. But then again, I've played it safe my whole life and what has it gotten me?

I lead Rosie into the crossties, run a brush over her coat, and then saddle her like Finn showed me.

Finn.

Picturing him in here brings back the way he made me feel when we kissed last night, and I suddenly miss him with a fierceness he doesn't deserve. But I'm confident I know how to put a saddle on this special horse, and I'm ready to ride, to leave my life behind, even for just a moment.

The bridle is trickier—there are a lot more straps and buckles, to say nothing of the bit—but because Rosie is my equine soulmate, she opens her mouth without me having to do the finger thing, and I manage to slip the bridle over her head.

By the time we make it outside, there are dark clouds overhead and they're moving in fast. But I don't care. All that matters is riding away from here until I'm too tired to think about Gigi and Dean and everything I've lost.

"You and me, girl," I tell Rosie. "We're going to get out of here for a bit. Who needs backstabbing best friends and princes we knew would break our heart, right? We've got each other."

She seems to snuffle in agreement as I lead her around to the mounting block. And like the perfect creature that she is, she stands stock-still as I climb the steps and awkwardly clamber into the saddle.

"Be good to me, will you?" I whisper as I take up the reins. My heart's still pounding, but I no longer feel scared. I feel powerful, and it's about damn time.

I squeeze her sides with my calves and she starts walking. As I feel more comfortable, I encourage her to speed up until she's trotting. My mind begins to clear. I murmur to her, thanking her for behaving so well and taking such good care of me. We head down to the meadow path and follow what I think is the same route that Finn and I took. But I'm paying more attention to my posting than I am to the scenery, and suddenly, we're in the woods. Except that it looks different than it did before. Is that just because of the clouds? Or because I took a wrong turn somewhere?

We're no longer on a trail, I realize. We're just trotting randomly through the trees.

I pull on the reins and Rosie slows to a walk. It's going to be okay. I just need to get my bearings. But because we've left the trail, I can't just turn around and backtrack. I have no idea which way we came from.

As I twist around in the saddle, scanning the woods for something I recognize, the first drops of rain hit me.

Everything looks the same. The sky darkens, the rain comes down harder, and I'm turning in circles.

"It's okay," I reassure myself as much as I'm reassuring Rosie. My wobbling voice betrays me. "We can figure this out."

The sky opens up and pours down on us like sheets, and suddenly I can't see anything at all.

16

I'm soaked through, from my head to my boots. My hands ache from clutching the reins. Guilt over subjecting sweet Rosie to this weather is taking me down. I'd be crying if I wasn't so cold and it didn't take so much effort.

I guide Rosie to a denser section of the woods where we can get at least a bit of shelter from the storm. I dismount, then keep walking, waiting for something to look familiar, waiting for a miracle. My miracle comes in the form of a stone cottage, about the size of my two-story home in Wisconsin.

Thankfully, it includes a smaller structure (likely once a carriage house) that's been converted into a stable. I apologize profusely to Rosie as I lead her into a stall, take off her bridle, and get her settled with water and hay.

Figuring the odds of a serial killer living on royal property, particularly one so bougie, are low, I approach the front door and knock. There aren't any lights on, so I try the handle. Bingo. I'm dripping rain all over the foyer of this house, but I don't care. I'm out of the elements and no longer feel like I'm going to die in some truly embarrassing way, which gives me perspective. I can stay here tonight, wherever "here" is, and hopefully find my way back to my own cottage in the morning. I hate myself for leaving my phone behind.

Rubbing my arms, teeth chattering, I explore what seems to be a hunting lodge that's still in regular use by the royal family. The horse supplies in the makeshift stable make sense now. The aged hardwood floor is covered in dark rugs. The furniture is sturdy leather with heavy oak tables and chairs here and there. The walls feature old-fashioned guns and taxidermic deer heads and stuffed birds. I make my way around, flicking on lights to help me get my bearings.

There's firewood on the back porch. I gather some dry pieces and bring them into the living room. My summers in Illinois have taught me the art of making a fire, and I fully intend to start one soon. But first, I peek into three different bedrooms in search of clothing. The first is a master bedroom. Not gonna touch anything there. I wander into another room that gives off Finn vibes, and not just because there's a trunk with his initials at the foot of the bed. In the dresser, I find a pair of sweatpants and a flannel shirt, but I'm not sure changing into them will be enough to warm me up. Still shivering and damp, what I really want is a hot shower.

I head into the en-suite, then hesitate. Am I really going to use a member of the royal family's shower without permission? After breaking into their house? *Which I accessed after taking their horse?!*

I'm so getting deported.

Oh well, at least my hair will look nice in my mug shot. This bathroom is stocked with top-tier hair products. I suppose those copper locks don't shine and fall the way they do by accident.

I step out of my wet clothes, hang them on the towel rack, and turn on the shower. It takes a while for the water to heat up, but it eventually does, eliciting a moan of relief from deep within me. I step into a shower that's big enough for two (not that it matters), the water shocking and stinging my frozen skin. To distract myself from the pain and calm myself from the fear of not knowing where the hell I am, I start singing. Being the world's most average singer has never stopped me from belting show tunes in the shower.

Warm and clean, I turn off the water and pat myself dry, all while continuing to sing my way through "One Day More" from *Les Mis.* I help myself to fancy face moisturizer and body lotion, in addition to the clothes I found. There's no way I'm putting my wet underwear and bra back on, but that hardly matters when here alone. Commando it is.

I blow-dry my hair until I get bored and then scrunch it with my hands to coax out my natural blond waves.

Ready to build that fire, I walk out of the bathroom, back into the bedroom, and immediately scream because I am *not*, in fact, alone.

"Has anyone ever told you that you should be on Broadway?" Finn asks from the bed where he's stretched out, hands behind his head, as though he doesn't have a care in the world. "I thought your karaoke performance was impressive, but *Les Mis*? Brava."

I grab the decorative pillow from a nearby chair and throw it at him. He catches it.

"What are you doing here?" I ask, still trying to slow down my racing heart that was momentarily convinced I was about to be murdered in the woods.

"In *my* hunting lodge?" He sits up. "I could ask you the same question, Goldilocks. By the way, how are you enjoying my hair products and clothing? Thank you for leaving me some things to wear so I could change out of my wet clothes too. Such a thoughtful little intruder."

Hah. So I was right about this room. "I have zero complaints," I say. I'm so relieved to see him, I have to fight the urge to leap onto the bed to hug him. Remembering that I'm furious with him helps smother the baser instinct. I level him with an icy stare. "Where's Beatrice? Is she here too? I'd love to meet her."

Finn sighs and rises from the bed. "Hannah, I owe you an apology. Multiple apologies. My family wasn't supposed to be back here for another month, and when I got the text that they were on their way, and I was to meet them at the private airport . . ." He tentatively takes my hands in his. "The timing couldn't have been worse."

I yank my hands away. "Why did you tell me things were over between you and Beatrice?"

"Because they were," he insists. "I mean, they *are.*"

"Interesting. Because you two were practically canoodling in back of the Rolls," I point out, wincing all over again at the humiliation I experienced when he looked at me as though he didn't even know me.

Technically, he and Beatrice weren't canoodling, they were just sitting next to each other, but Finn doesn't correct me. Instead, he sits on the edge of the bed and runs his fingers through his hair. There's a part of me that wants to run my fingers through his hair too. I'm clearly a glutton for punishment.

"Bringing Beatrice was a 'fun little surprise,' courtesy of my parents. I swear to you, I don't want her here. I don't want her at all."

"What *do* you want?" I ask before I can stop myself.

"*You,*" he says.

That's all I needed to hear. I reach out to feel the silky, slightly damp waves of his hair, combing my fingers through, giving the slightest of tugs when I reach the ends. He lets out a small hum at my touch and my belly turns to liquid.

"Is there any way," he asks, his voice low, "that I can kiss you again and this time, I promise not to run away, abandoning you in a dark alley?"

"The words every girl dreams of hearing." My breath catches in my throat because he's standing now, coming closer.

But I can't let him have the upper hand. Not just yet.

Beside the canopy bed are two engraved wooden steps, beautiful *and* functional, since the bed is too high for me to get into gracefully. I take his fingers, linking them through mine, and step up until we are nearly eye to eye.

"Well, now, that's an even better view of you," he says, nuzzling my jaw with his chin. His hands grip my waist, and I inhale the scent of him while I run my fingers through his hair again. Just when I think this moment can't feel any more intimate, his lips find mine. I part them for him, welcoming his heat, his tongue, his affection. My breasts press against his chest, sending a charge through me. I want more of him, more of this. Kissing Finn feels like being worshipped. I want to know how everything else with him will feel.

His hands run down to cup my bottom and I wrap my legs around him. Carefully, so carefully he doesn't even break our kiss, he lays me onto the bed. When I'm on the softest mattress I've ever experienced, only then does he pull away. With one finger, he delicately brushes away a lock of hair from my face.

"My beautiful, perfect Hannah."

The best word out of all of them is "my."

"I was so worried, so . . ." His eyes cast down, the fringe of his auburn eyelashes in full view.

I take his hand and hold it. "About what?"

"You disappeared," he says as though it's obvious. *Oh yeah. That.* "Knowing what it looked like to see me drive up with Beatrice, no word of warning, I got away as soon as I could. You weren't at your cottage. I looked all over the grounds and when I realized Rosie was gone too, all I could think was . . ."

"I'm sorry," I say, warmed by the intensity of his concern. "What I did was *really* stupid. I'm sorry I made you worry."

"I'm sorry I upset you," he says. "I'm just glad you're okay. And so are these wide doe eyes. This pouty mouth. These flushing cheeks." He places tender kisses on every part he names.

"Is that all?" I tease. "What do you think of my ears?" When he rolls off me, I regret my glibness and try to pull him toward me. "Where are you going?"

"I want to say something to you. Something important."

He's lying on his back now. I scooch closer until the sides of our bodies are aligned and we're both staring at the vaulted ceiling and the dark beams running across it. When his hand finds mine, our fingers lace together as though this is what they've always done. What they'll always do.

"You remember Tina? My prison warden you met in the stables?"

"Of course."

"I've known Tina since I was a boy. When my sister Poppy was a toddler and I was about five, and James and Amelia were busy with their overly scheduled lives, Tina would take the two of us into the garden to catch ladybugs. We'd have this little crate that Poppy and I would decorate with leaves and sticks and grass, all manner of things we thought the ladybugs would like, and then we'd put the little red bugs in there and let them make friends with one another. We'd always set them free afterwards. Poppy worried the ladybugs wouldn't be happy cooped up. Tina seemed to understand that Poppy and I weren't happy cooped up either. Looking after us, she didn't care if I got mud on my trousers or if Poppy's plaits came loose. But when Mum and Dad returned home from whatever philanthropic venture they were tending to, we'd be back in shipshape, reading quietly in the study."

"She must be protective of you," I say, trying to reconcile the severe woman I met while in a semi-compromising position with the one Finn's describing.

He nods, his thumb tracing my hand, my wrist. "Because of her, I've always had a keen sense for people who have my best interests at heart. It's difficult to trust people—and, yes, I know that's not an affliction borne solely by those in the public eye."

My mind automatically goes to Gigi and Dean, and my body tenses in response. He holds my hand more tightly, caressing it with his thumb. "It's not," I say. "But you definitely see it in a more concentrated form than most people."

He rolls onto his side and surveys me. "When we first met, I admit the first thing that appealed to me was your smart mouth and the scent of the chase. But after seeing you crying in the alleyway after losing your job, after messaging with you and spending time with you here . . .

"You have the loveliest heart, Hannah. The sweetest soul." He shakes his head with a smile. "I know I sound like I'm reciting the cheesiest boy band lyrics of all time, but I mean it. I see your goodness just as clearly as I see your beauty, feel your humor, see your strength—god, how many people could go to a different continent at eighteen, have their summer plans flipped, and then thrive with the changes?"

I've never been referred to as "strong" before. I'm trying on the word, getting comfortable with it. And I'm seeing myself through his eyes. Being with Finn isn't just making me fall for him, it's making me like myself more.

"Thank you," I say, scratching the stubble on his jaw.

He lets out an exaggerated sigh and rolls his eyes. "Now would be the time when you shower *me* with compliments. God, Hannah."

I grin and pull him on top of me, nibbling at his ear and

neck to make him squirm. He tickles my ribs in response and we both laugh. Eventually, we find ourselves holding each other as our breaths slow.

"You're very swoonable," I say, kissing along his jaw.

I can feel the muscles of his smile against my mouth. "'Swoonable.' Is that even a word?"

"If Shakespeare's allowed to invent seventeen hundred words, I'm allowed to invent at least one."

"Well, then, I think you're very swoonable too," he says, and then all our words, real and created, get lost in a kiss.

17

We alternate between kissing and talking for the rest of the night. At some point, we move down to the living room, where we argue about which of us is the best fire builder, then move the couch closer to the flames and listen to the storm outside. We're snuggled under a warm, woolen tartan blanket, already entangled and yet still finding excuses to touch each other, to explore. I wriggle my toes underneath him because they're cold; he tucks my hair behind my shoulder anytime it blocks his view of my face.

Finn tells me more about his summers here. I listen to stories about Tina's kindness to him and his siblings and the way Ethel has looked out for them over the years. When he asks me why I took Rosie out in the first place, I admit to breaking my self-induced social media hiatus.

"After seeing you and Beatrice roll up, I decided to torture myself a little more and scrolled through Gigi's and Dean's posts."

"Do you miss him?" I can tell he's trying to sound understanding, but if I answer yes, it might break him.

"I don't," I say, and clock the relief in his face. "I do miss Gigi, though. As mad as I am at her. That betrayal feels deeper than Dean's."

"Have you spoken to her?" When I shake my head, he adds, "It's worth considering. Even if you never forgive her, it might help you if you get the full picture, hear her side of it."

"Maybe." But I know I'm not ready for that. Not yet. The room is quiet, but for the crackling of the fire. "The storm is over," I muse.

"Well, that's a shame. I was ready to stay here forever."

"Me too," I admit. He leans over and kisses me again, achingly slow. When we finally pull apart, I note the early-morning light filtering through the window. "How long can a prince go missing before it's declared an international incident?"

Finn glances at the window. "'It is not yet near day: It was the nightingale, and not the lark.'"

"I'm sorry, what?"

"It's what Juliet tells Romeo after their first night together, when she doesn't want him to leave."

"And you mocked me for using the word 'rapscallion'? Hypocrite."

The fire is dying. I push it around until it's out while Finn tidies up the room and retrieves my almost-dry clothes. When I'm dressed, he extends a hand. "Shall we?"

"Nah. I'm still Team Stay Here and Let the World Freak Out." But I take his hand, and we walk outside.

Despite the fact that I barely slept, I feel fully awake the moment the air hits my skin. I take a deep breath, relishing the crisp, piney scent. Spicier and more pungent than a Christmas tree, but with hints of the nearby sea. I close my eyes, inhale again, and say, "If you could bottle this scent and sell it, you'd make a million dollars."

"I'll keep that in mind the next time we come up short on the rent."

"Well, forgive me, Mr. Eleventh-Richest Person in Britain."

"Surely I've dropped to at least eighteenth by now." He counts off on his fingers. "There's that chap who founded the AI company, and that actress with that app. And I think Richard Branson has had quite a good year."

We fetch the horses from the stable and ride back at a leisurely pace. It's clear that neither of us is in a rush to return to real life. Curls of mist cling to the trees, birds chitter in the distance, and the world feels somehow both fresh and ancient. How many generations of Finn's ancestors have galloped down this path? How many knights thundered off to battle? How many princesses rode through these trees to be handed off to their betrothed?

"The castle's closed to the public today," he reminds me. "What are your plans?"

I shrug. A bit shyly, I tell him about the book I'm writing. "I'm going to try to get a few chapters down."

Finn looks thrilled. "That's wonderful. Can I read it when it's ready?"

The question presumes not only that I'm going to finish it, but a future between us. My heart flutters in my chest. I nod. "Sure. What about you? What are your plans?"

"Oh, I'm sure my parents have filled the diary with various activities to keep me out of trouble." We emerge from the woods into the meadow and Finn turns Ivanhoe in a circle. It's clear he's getting antsy, unaccustomed to staying on a walk for this long.

"Well, if you have a spare moment," I say suggestively, "the cozy cottage I'm living in would welcome you."

"As soon as I can get away, I will."

The stables are still quiet when we reach them. A young man is unloading bales of hay from a flatbed truck, and a woman is hosing down the drive. They both nod respectfully at Finn as we approach, then return to their tasks.

We dismount and lead the horses inside to untack them. "Thank you," I whisper to Rosie as I give her coat a final brush. "You're a literal lifesaver." In response, she nuzzles my shoulder.

I assume Finn will want to play it cool now that there are people around, but as we head toward the stable door, he pulls me to him and kisses me once, twice, and then lingers on the third.

"Goodbye for now, my American Hannah," he says, placing one more kiss on my forehead.

My arms are around his waist. I hold him tightly, not wanting to let him go. Alas, real life calls. I release him and give him time to walk out first. In case any of the groundskeeping staff are around, I wait in the stables for a few minutes before leaving myself. While I'm stalling, I mentally relive the best night of my life. I know I'm falling for Finn at lightning speed, and it scares the hell out of me. But it also thrills me. No one has made me feel like he does on any level—not physically, not emotionally. After what happened with Dean, I was certain I'd never trust another guy again. Yet Finn makes trusting him easy.

My stomach is growling, demanding breakfast. I figure I've given Finn enough of a head start. Gingerly, I step outside. I look toward the castle to ensure no one's about and come face-to-face with Tina.

"Hi, good morning," I say as nonchalantly as I can, trying to recover from the gasp of alarm that came out first.

Instead of returning my greeting, she continues to appraise my disheveled appearance with her steely gray eyes. I am sure she's registering the fact that the sun hasn't even completely risen, I'm far away from the servants' quarters, and I'm wearing Finn's plaid shirt over my own.

"You've been spending a lot of time with the prince," she says carefully.

"We're friends." In an attempt to distract her or ingratiate myself to her—or both—I add, "He speaks so highly of you."

Her mouth forms a thin line. Despite what Finn has said, I still find this woman terrifying and I'm anxious to get out of here.

"I just wanted to say hi to Rosie," I say quickly. "I brought her some carrots."

The tone of her response stops me cold. "I do hope you two left the hunting lodge in an acceptable manner. I would hate for it to appear as though something untoward had occurred there."

"I . . ." I'm trying to come up with a response, with *anything*, as her stare intensifies. I want to shrivel up and roll down the hill, never to be seen or heard from again. "We . . ."

"In any other circumstance, the dalliances of a young man would be no business of mine. But he isn't just a young man, Hannah, as you well know." She raises her chin. "He's a leader and a legacy. I recognize that you haven't been raised in a country that understands the gravity of this."

"I understand—" I try to say, but she cuts me off.

"You would do well to be careful. Nothing in his highness's life is simple or inconsequential. Nothing can be treated as such."

I won't break his heart, I want to tell her, but I know that's the least of Tina's worries. As much as she cares about him, chances are she's thinking about foreign affairs and paparazzi.

"Noted," I say instead. "I should go."

"Yes," she agrees.

When I get back to my cottage, I have something to eat, then crawl into bed and try to sleep, but it's useless.

I growl and throw my pillow across my bed. I immediately feel guilty, since these aren't technically my belongings, and I stand up to retrieve it. To distract myself, I start straightening up my cottage. Since there's only a kitchen, a living room/bedroom, and a small bathroom, it doesn't take nearly long enough. I remind myself of my goals and grab my laptop to work on my book. After typing out three paragraphs and deleting two, my phone rings. I grab it, hoping it's Finn.

The caller ID says *Gigi.* The temptation to send her straight to voicemail is there and it's potent. I'm frozen, staring at the phone. I remember what Finn said last night about how talking to her doesn't mean I have to forgive her, but it might help. I press the green button and say nothing.

"Hannah?" The voice of my former best friend is as familiar as my own. Tears prickle the corners of my eyes, despite my silent demands that they stop.

"Yeah," I finally reply. I hate that she'll be able to tell that I'm crying. She knows me that well.

"How—how are you?" She sounds incredibly nervous. There's no way she expected me to answer.

I can't do this. I can't handle small talk. If we're going to do this, fine, but then we're actually going to talk.

"How did it start?" I don't have to clarify. She knows what I'm asking.

There's a pause. "Um, I guess—"

"No," I cut her off. "Don't *guess*. You know how it started, so just tell me."

I can hear her sniffle. I picture her in her bedroom, decorated with volleyball trophies and art she's picked out over the years from random garage sales. We've had countless sleepovers in that room. And I'll never enter it again.

"It was when you weren't allowed to go to that bush party because your grandparents were in town," Gigi eventually says. "Dean gave me a ride to be nice. He and I had never hung out before, just the two of us, without you there, and . . ."

Her voice trails off. I'm picturing everything. Gigi and her impossibly long dark hair, her lashes that are so thick and full that mascara is made redundant. Gigi's spontaneous and wild and does things without thinking, which can be frustrating, but it's also what makes her fun. For our entire lives, she's pulled me out of my shell while I've grounded her. We've balanced each other.

For one night, though, I wasn't there to do that, and she let her wild side take control.

"What happened at the party?" I prompt.

"You know me," she says with an embarrassed laugh. "I got drunk and stupid."

"And Dean took advantage of that? Of you being drunk and stupid?" Dean may have turned out to be a cheating toolbag, but he's still a decent human being; the guy knows what consent is. If I was even a little buzzed when I was out with him, he'd give me one chaste kiss and take me home.

"No. Of course he didn't." Gigi stops and sniffles some more. "Okay, I wasn't drunk. I had half a beer. I was just stupid."

"For god's sake, G, tell me the truth, or what's even the point of this fucking phone call?"

Silence.

I consider hanging up. But if I do, then all I've accomplished is making us both miserable. I deserve answers, even if I'm not going to like them.

"It was at the beginning of the night." This time when Gigi talks, her voice is quiet. Resigned. "Nicki was blabbing about the time we played some dumb kissing game at her house when we were, like, twelve, and then everyone was joking about playing a kissing game right then. Dean was worried about getting caught up in it, so he said he was going to walk down to the river, and I said I'd go with him."

"Were you planning on kissing him?" I squeeze my eyes shut, imagining it all. Seeing it in my mind, hearing her say it hurts. It's like all the scar tissue I've worked so hard to develop is being poked and prodded.

"No! God no," she assures me. "I always thought you guys were cute and wished I had someone like Dean, but I didn't set out to, like, seduce him or anything."

"Does it matter if you had planned it?" I say as much to myself as to Gigi. "You two may not have snuck away to secretly make out, but you both chose to carry on behind my back for the better part of a year. *That* took planning."

"But, Hannah, you have to know—"

Suddenly, I don't want to hear any more. "You can stop. I've had enough."

"But . . ." Gigi hiccups. "You haven't forgiven me."

"You haven't even said that you're sorry." Then I hang up.

I sit there, staring at my phone for who knows how long. A heaviness sinks in my chest. In some twisted way, that horrible phone call unknotted my mind. I don't feel better—in fact, in some ways, I feel worse. Still, I faced what I've been hiding from for weeks, and that's worth something.

There's only one person I want to talk to about this, even though I know texting him right now is risky. I send Finn a message.

I answered a phone call from Gigi. I heard her out and lived to tell the tale. It was terrible and I'm glad I did it. Thank you for encouraging me to stop hiding from her.

I wait, but no response comes.

18

Since Inveresk Castle is still closed to the public while the royal family is here and I get a day off, I text Finn and suggest we meet later to go riding. After a power nap, I try a writing trick my English teacher taught me called free-falling. The key is to write immediately, as soon as you wake up, before you're alert enough to edit yourself and second-guess yourself. I'm able to get two thousand words on the page before I need to get ready to see Finn. And I even like a lot of those words. I can't wait to tell him about my breakthrough.

I shower and dress, thinking about how lucky I am to get to ride two days in a row. I walk to the stables, Finn on my mind and in my heart. My imagination wanders to X-rated places, making me flush. Thankfully, a breeze kicks up to cool me off just as the stable hands wave to me. They're tending to the ponies outside, which means Finn will be inside alone.

"Hi," I practically sing, the now-familiar smell of hay greeting me. Finn is in the midst of saddling up Ivanhoe. When he turns to look at me, I don't quite get the greeting I'm expecting. He doesn't say hello. He doesn't say anything and I can't quite read his expression.

"Oh, are you a new stable hand?" a posh British voice says.

Beatrice, the woman I've cyber-stalked every day since I learned of her existence, is approaching me. I'm finally seeing her up close and personal. Predictably, she is perfection in tailored, fawn-colored breeches that hug her tiny but still well-formed rear, navy cashmere sweater, and shiny black riding boots. Her dark hair is pulled up and sleek. It's all I can do not to run away in my beat-up jeans, crop top, and sneakers. I've never felt so short and squat in my life.

"Stable hand?" I repeat.

"This is Hannah," Finn corrects her. "I told you about my American friend who's working at the gift shop this summer."

"It's nice to meet you," I say automatically, even if it isn't the truth. I keep my eyes fixed on Beatrice, too afraid of what I'll see in Finn's face if I look.

"Oh, of course. The American friend, *Hannah.*" She steps forward, and to my amazement, air-kisses me on both cheeks. "I hear Finn saved you from abject poverty."

I'm so taken aback, I don't think before replying, "I'm pretty sure I saved him from abject boredom."

She lets out a laugh that I'm sure is fake, though it's convincing enough.

Finn clears his throat. "Shall we be off?"

Ah. So this riding excursion now includes the guy I'm falling for and his hot ex. Wonderful.

I'm already feeling sharply territorial about Finn, and that jealousy extends to my horse soulmate. Pretending I'm totally cool with every single thing happening in here, I ask, "Who are you riding, Beatrice? Rosie?"

Beatrice gives me a perfect toothpaste-commercial smile. "Oh, no. She's better suited to beginners, isn't she? I'll be on Puck. So you are, in fact . . . joining us on the ride, Hannah?"

It feels as though I've just fallen into a pond in November. I'm the interloper here, not Beatrice. I redden as she continues to stare at me in consternation.

"I've been giving Hannah riding lessons," Finn explains. "What do you think, Hannah? Would you like to join us?"

"Please do, Hannah. I insist. Any friend of Finn's, well . . . *almost* any friend of Finn's," Beatrice says. The two of them share a laugh over some private joke as she greets a dark horse that looks like Ivanhoe's twin and, quite frankly, scares the hell out of me.

I'm tempted to run back to the cottage and spend the day hiding from this British goddess. But the fact that she probably doesn't want me here, coupled with the fact that I know Finn does, makes me dig in my heels.

"Sure, I'll join you."

"Wonderful," Finn says. I hope I'm not imagining the relief in his voice.

"Wonderful," Beatrice echoes. She gives me a tight smile. "Puck and Ivanhoe are brothers, you know."

"Fascinating," I say, trying to keep the sarcasm out of my voice. If this is some weird horse-adjacent way of telling me she's better suited for Finn, I don't care.

When Finn asks me if I need help getting on Rosie, I swear I hear a titter from Beatrice. Reddening, I assure him I can do it.

"Sorry, it was unavoidable," he whispers in my ear before stepping back to allow me to mount Rosie. I nod and blessedly manage to get on the horse without humiliating myself.

Like Finn, Beatrice mounts without using the block. I don't know much about horses, but it seems like she stuck her butt out more than necessary before hoisting herself into the saddle. To my dismay, she looks even more elegant astride Puck than she did on the ground. The three of us set out, and as we reach the end of the drive, Beatrice calls out, "Finneas? The usual?"

It's an innocent comment, and yet I can't help but feel as though it's also designed to make me feel out of place. *Well, I'm already a common foreigner hanging out at a castle in Scotland, babe. I can take your little jabs.*

"Sure. The usual," he calls back to her.

Finn catches my attention to give me another apologetic look. I keep my face neutral and ignore it. I'm not angry with him. Finn has obligations outside our growing relationship that I barely understand. Who knows, maybe pissing off Beatrice somehow starts a war in Finland or something.

Beatrice rises into the stirrups, leans forward slightly, and Puck takes off at gallop. It's like watching a sports car go from zero to sixty in three seconds. Ivanhoe whinnies and tosses his head, eager to follow suit, but Finn keeps him at a steady trot next to me.

"She was supposed to attend a luncheon at some philanthropic something or other with Mother and Poppy," Finn explains when she's out of earshot. "At the last minute, Mother convinced her to go riding with me instead."

"It's okay," I say. And it really is. If it means spending time with him, I'll put up with an ice queen. Or ice duchess, or whatever her title is. "Maybe we can hang out later? Just us?"

"My father's insomnia is the only obstacle I have to deal with in the evenings. Providing he's not roaming the castle halls tonight, I'll come tap at your window." We stare at each other, the heat building between us. "I want to kiss you," he says.

"There are a lot of things I'd like to do with you. Maybe behind that tree," I reply, vaguely surprised at how brazen

I'm being. I've never said anything like that to anyone, not even Dean. But with Finn . . .

His eyes turn molten. "I want to—"

We're interrupted by the sound of pounding hooves. I look up just in time to see Beatrice steer Puck toward an enormous fallen log. He leaps over it easily and gallops straight toward us. My heart begins to pound. What if she runs into us? Will Rosie take off? Or will we just get trampled? As I brace for impact, Beatrice leans back slightly and Puck comes to an abrupt stop. "Everything all right?" she asks with mock concern. "I've never seen you ride so slowly in your life."

"I should head home," I say. "I'm holding you both back."

"Hannah, please stay," Finn pleads.

"Truly, it's okay. I've got some writing to do."

"If you're certain." His eyes are trying to read me and I let them, because I really am certain. Interfering with Beatrice's plans was fun for a moment or two, but I have no desire to spend the day with her.

"By the way, Hannah," Beatrice calls before I leave. "We're going to the Highland games and then to the beach to view the aurora borealis tomorrow. You must join us."

"Oh," I say in surprise. I'm not terribly interested in another third-wheel situation (who the third wheel is, is unclear). But I don't want to miss out on the chance to spend more time with Finn. "Who's going?"

"Some of Finneas's closest friends are coming for a visit." She looks at me expectantly. "Tell me you'll come too. After all, aren't you in charge of making sure Finneas doesn't get bored?"

"Right. Yes, I'd love to," I say. What she doesn't know is I've already met Callum, Mhairi, and Bethany, so I'm not intimidated in the least.

"Wonderful," she replies with a smile that looks as insincere as mine feels.

19

In my dream, there's a woodpecker who will not shut up. The stupid bird is pecking against the walls of my room until it gets stuck in my chimney and is absolutely relentless.

"*Hannah,*" the woodpecker says.

I shoot straight up in bed and open my eyes. There's no tenacious bird outside my door, but there is a very sexy prince who's trying to get my attention. I climb out of bed and open my front door. Finn, who is wearing dark slacks and a button-up shirt open at the collar, slips in.

"Either you were debating whether or not you wanted to see me or you're a very deep sleeper," he says.

"The latter." I flick on a light and immediately recoil from the brightness, which makes him laugh. His laughter stops short.

"Now *this* is an alluring little getup," he says, blatantly drinking in my appearance.

I'm wearing short-shorts and an oversized crewneck sweater. Not what I would consider sexy at all.

"I will never understand the hetero male mind." I turn off the overhead light and switch to a lamp that's much less abrasive. Now that I'm awake, I'm giddy he's here. I shuffle to him and wrap my arms around his waist, breathing him in. His arms instantly welcome me. He holds me tight, placing a kiss on the top of my head.

"I've missed you," he said. "I'm sorry about this afternoon. Beatrice—"

"I've missed you too." I cut him off because I don't want to talk about his ex-girlfriend right now. I involuntarily shiver because the floor is cold on my feet and my legs were under blankets mere moments ago.

"I'm sorry I woke you up." He pulls away to look at me, a lopsided grin on his face. "Though perhaps not *that* sorry."

"Come get under the covers with me." I lead him to my bed and we both climb in. It's a twin, so we have to get really close to fit, which suits me just fine.

His arms are around me, my head on his chest, and the quilt is pulled up. I feel so safe and comfortable, the stressful events of the day feel like they happened a lifetime ago: my call with Gigi, the agony of seeing perfect Beatrice in real life.

As if reading my mind, Finn strokes my hair and says, "You still haven't told me about your conversation with Gigi."

I relay the phone call, including the part where I hung up. I try to keep my voice steady, but by the end, I feel tears threatening again. Finn kisses the top of my head again and gives me a squeeze.

"That must've been hard. But you're glad you did it?"

I sit up so I can see him better. We lean against the bed frame. He takes my hand and intertwines our fingers, a now familiar tradition when we're close.

"I am. Avoiding her was becoming its own monster. Now that I've faced that initial call, I don't have to hide from her anymore. Not that she's going to call again." I know Gigi well enough to know that. She'll turn her attention away from me and toward volleyball, toward starting college in the fall. We chose schools that are within an easy driving distance of each other, but we can just as easily not make that drive too. "I'm going to miss her, though. Miss what we had." Saying it out loud pushes a tear to the edge and down my cheek.

Finn leans over and kisses it away. "I'm so sorry this happened to you. You are brilliantly kind and good. You don't deserve it."

Being with him feels so right, but it's battling against Tina's warning: *You would do well to be careful.* And that's on top of the distant alarm bells I've never been fully able to silence in my own mind, a constant reminder that whatever Finn and I have, whatever's going on between us, it has an expiration date.

"What's going on with you and Queen Bea?" I ask suddenly.

"Referring to someone as 'queen' who isn't royalty is a punishable offense at Inveresk Castle." Finn's tone is light, but I can tell he's irritated by the question. "Are you really worried about her?"

I tap my chin. "Am I worried about the tall, lithe goddess who you planned on marrying and is now living under the same roof as you . . . hmm . . ."

"Hannah." He takes my hand and kisses it. "I had no idea having her here was bothering you this much. I apologize. Truly. If I could kick her out—well, it'd be rude because she's my friend—but I'd do it anyway to please you."

"You don't have to kick her out." I snuggle in closer to him, reminding myself that he's here with me. He snuck out to be with *me.* Any restlessness I had as a result of our three's-company ride dissolves. When Tina's stern face appears in my head again, I swat it away. *I'm tired of being careful,* I tell her. *Being careful has gotten me nowhere. I want to stop following a plan and start following my feelings.* "Thank you for coming here tonight," I tell him, leaning forward to pepper his neck with soft kisses. I move up and catch his earlobe between my teeth, and he moans in response.

"That's very swoonable, what you're doing there," he says.

I laugh into his skin. "See? My made-up word is catching on."

My hand moves down his chest and stomach, which flexes in response. I get close to the waistband of his pants, and he lets out a breath. The anticipation building between us creates a heady, intoxicating chemistry. I run my hands back up his chest, pressing myself against him. Everything in my body, from the top of my head to my toes, is tingling with want. He catches my lips with his, our mouths opening. Heat passes between us. I reach down to see just how much he's enjoying this attention. Before I get there, I ask if it's okay. He affirms that it's more than okay, and he pushes himself against my hand. I'm so turned on, I'm lightheaded. I want everything, all of him.

When his hands rake down my back, squeezing my bottom, and then tucking underneath my thigh, I freeze. He instantly stops and pulls away.

"Are you okay?" he says. His hands are off me, his voice full of tenderness. "We can just talk, if you want."

I want to do more; I want everything, but.

Heat rises up my chest, my neck. I'm certain it's blotting my cheeks.

"You can tell me anything," he coaxes. "Or nothing, it's up to you. I can even leave, if that's what you want."

I grab his wrist. "No, I want you here, I want to touch you and be touched, I just . . . I have to warn you about something before we do more."

"Is it that you have extra toes?" he says with a serious nod. "That's more common than you'd think."

I laugh, and the tension building in me breaks. I'm just going to be honest with him.

"I've never . . ." *I will not hide my face, I'm just going to say it.* "Climaxed with a partner before."

"Oh," he says, taking the information in. There's no judgment in his voice. If anything, there's a curiosity. "And that's something you'd like to experience."

"Yeah." I bite my lower lip, thinking how best to put into words something I've never said out loud before. "I've only been with one person and every time we hooked up, I'd be having a good time, then get in my head about it. The whole thing frustrated him and embarrassed me, and I just don't want to have that come between us." I gather the courage to meet his eye.

"This became a point of conflict?" he asks carefully.

"Kind of." I try not to think about how this must've made Gigi so much more appealing. She's always been free and shameless in her pursuit of pleasure.

"Well, then, he's a complete wanker," Finn says with more bitterness than I'm expecting. "The guy can't meet your needs and then makes you feel bad about it?"

"Well, it's my fault too, though," I say.

"But you can climax by yourself," Finn clarifies. When I nod, he throws up his hands. "Nope, I'm sorry, Hannah, the verdict is, he's a wad and you deserve to feel better than you've ever felt."

While the conversation may not necessarily be sexy, his

reaction to it absolutely is. Rather than say this to him, I push him back and straddle him. I rock my hips a little to create friction, which makes his eyes roll back.

"Oh my god, Hannah."

This physical experience, the sight of him turned on, it's all working for me. I ride him for a little longer, taking his shirt off in the process. I declare his body swoonable, and then he places his hands on my hips and stills me.

"Something wrong?" I ask.

"Yes," he says. "We're going to take care of you first. I don't care if I have to dedicate the rest of my life to this very valuable cause."

"It might take a while. It might not even happen," I warn him.

"But won't it be fun to try?" he replies with a wicked grin. He flips me onto my back, his hands at the hem of my sweatshirt. "May I?"

I nod, already feeling my body buzz and build with the anticipation of his effect on me. His hands reach up to fondle my breasts as he plants gentle kisses on my stomach. It feels so good, but it's not enough.

"*More*," I murmur.

His kisses travel down to my hip bone. As his hands trace under the waistband of my shorts, he looks up to make sure I'm on board. I'm so on board, I whip the shorts off myself. He hums in appreciation as his mouth travels inside my thigh. I beg him this time. *"More."*

It doesn't take all night. It doesn't even take an hour for Finn to bring me to the peak and back down again.

"Your turn," I whisper into his ear. I take him in my hands, my mouth, and then climb on top of him again to ride the friction.

When ecstasy comes, it comes for both of us, and it is spectacular.

My head falls onto the pillow; Finn's rests on my chest. My fingers comb through his hair as our bodies ride out the aftershocks until they're replaced with the sweet glow of satisfaction.

20

I've never been someone to agonize over what to wear. My wardrobe is full of decent basics and all the tops essentially go with any of the bottoms. But preparing for a full day with Beatrice, who's sure to look stunningly put together, has me on edge.

"Maybe you could just talk to your father. You know, tell him he needs to start doing something about his attitude," my mom whispers into the phone—and not for the first time.

I've got my AirPods in so I can talk to her and lay out different outfit possibilities at the same time. It doesn't help that my laundry is piling up and I'm running low on everything.

"Mom, I'm not going to give Dad a lecture on his attitude," I say. There's no bite to my refusal. I try to change the topic. "Would you like to know how things are going here?"

My mom ignores the question and keeps talking. "It's just, I asked him if he wanted to go for a walk and he looked at me like my head was on backwards. I'm trying to spend time with him. I make all this effort and he—"

"So I'm living in a castle now," I say, to shut her up.

"Oh, you are not," Mom says and clucks her tongue. I text her a selfie I took while standing in the parterre, Inveresk Castle behind me. She's still not buying it. "Looks like a great place to visit before you go back to that apartment Margaret MacIntyre got you in town."

"Margaret MacIntyre moved to Japan to be with her boyfriend. I work in a gift shop now." Is it partially my fault for not offering my parents this information sooner or is it wholly their fault for being too self-absorbed to ask me about my day when they call? Who knows. All I know is it feels good to punish her a little by dropping these like bombs on her monologue complaining about my dad.

"Well—well—" my mom stammers before gathering her wits and the only explanation that allows her to see herself as the perfect mom. "You always have been one to land on your feet. Speaking of which, Dean came by to drop off some of your belongings. A sweater and a Jane Austen book, I think. I didn't really peek in the bag. I swear I saw Gigi in his truck, but she didn't come in and didn't wave back at me. Are she and Dean friends still? That's a little strange, isn't it?"

My mom obviously knows that Dean and I broke up. What she doesn't know is why.

"They could be hooking up for all I care," I say, ignoring the pinch in my heart I still can't shake when I think about Gigi. "I gotta go. I'm heading to the Highland games with the prince of England."

"Sure you are," Mom says. "Hey, next time you talk to your dad, maybe you can sugge—"

"Bye, Mom." I hang up the phone before she gets worked up about my dad's so-called attitude again. I stare at my clothing options, mutter "This is stupid" to myself, and grab one of my summer dresses at random.

I'm in the back of a sleek black car, seated beside Finn's sister Penelope, facing him and Beatrice. Finn and I both seem to be trying not to look at each other for too long, an unspoken agreement that we're keeping whatever's happening between us under wraps. But, god, does he look handsome. He's wearing a crisp white dress shirt rolled up at the sleeves with two buttons undone at his neck. The pièce de résistance is the kilt. An actual *kilt.* I'm refusing to look at it for fear I'll get too turned on by the memory of the hunting lodge—not to mention the even hotter hookup in my cottage last night. With a kilt, we're talking easy access right now. Heat rises up my neck.

"I love your trainers," Penelope tells me. Although Finn calls her "Poppy," Beatrice doesn't, so I'm erring on the side of formality. She's about a year younger than I am, but the way she seems to take note of everyone and everything around her makes me think she's an old-soul kind of girl.

"Thanks," I say, lifting my toes up to try and see what she likes about my pale pink Chucks. "Your shoe collection would put mine to shame, though, I bet."

"I'd give them all up to be able to wear trainers with a dress," Penelope says with a sigh. "But my mother thinks it's 'common.'"

I catch Finn's eye and he's holding back a smile. I look away before I do something untoward, like leap across the back of this car to throw my arms around him.

"How are you enjoying working in the gift shop, Hannah?" Beatrice asks, smoothing the pleats on her own kilt.

I very much want to hate her, but, apart from mistaking me for a stable hand, she's been nice enough to me. And the way she's asking about work doesn't make me feel less than—she sounds genuinely curious. I chalk it up to the impeccable manners that come with a bougie upbringing. Although, it occurs to me that if Finn's been friends with her his whole life and fell in love with her, she must be a good person.

"The gift shop's good," I tell her. "My coworker is a lot of fun."

"Caro?" she asks eagerly. "I love her. She has the coolest

hair. One time, I overheard her tell one of the maids that she thinks I have real style. It sounded like she meant it."

"Of course she meant it. You clearly do have style." She's paired her kilt with an apricot-colored short-sleeved mock turtleneck and brown boots I'm coveting, despite not normally caring about shoes. "Hey, is it okay that I don't have anything tartan on? I don't want to anger the locals. Some of them are going to be chucking trees today."

"I have something you can use." Penelope reaches into her purse and pulls out a beautiful tartan silk scarf. Because the sundress I'm wearing is white, the greens and blues will really pop. "May I?"

I nod and Penelope wraps the scarf around me in a semi-complicated way. When she shows me how it looks in her pocket mirror, I grin. "Thank you. Now I'm *slightly* less likely to embarrass you all."

The event technically starts with a parade in the town's center, but Finn and Penelope are prohibited by their security from going. Instead, the car takes the four of us straight to the field where the bulk of the games will be taking place.

Beatrice and I get out of the car first (she more gracefully than I) and we immediately move aside to give photographers ample view of the prince and princess. It doesn't take more than a few seconds for a crowd to form. Security keeps them at a safe distance, and everyone seems respectful, but a number of people are already taking photos of

Finn and his sister. A few even aim their phones at me and Beatrice.

God, this is awkward. I'm sure everyone is wondering what this random girl is doing with them.

As I shift my weight from side to side, trying to feign interest in the nearby tent selling Scotch pies, haggis and gravy, and bacon baps, I glance at Beatrice, who looks perfectly poised.

Finn jogs over to tell us he has to give a quick speech to start off the games. He sets off, flagged by two security officers. It's so easy to forget who Finn is to the world when I get caught up in who he is to me.

Finn steps onto a makeshift stage and I can feel a surge of energy crackle in the crowd. "Good afternoon, East Lothian," he says into a microphone. He's confident and looks every bit the part of a prince at the Highland games. My heart bursts with pride at his charisma up there. "I am so pleased—as a member of the Highland games board, an enthusiast of the events, and, let's be honest, a man who fancies himself stronger than he actually is—to be here with you."

The audience gives him an appreciative laugh. I see one muscly guy in a kilt and a tank top flex for his significant other.

"As most of you know, the Highland games can be traced back to the time of the clans in the eleventh century. It was part of Scotland's culture for hundreds of years, but in the nineteenth century, it almost disappeared altogether. It was the dedication of my ancestor, Queen Victoria, who fell in love with Scotland on her honeymoon with Albert, who brought them back. She revived them in 1832, and they've grown in strength and popularity since then."

I applaud along with the rest of the audience, feeling an unexpected kinship with the late Queen Victoria. How can someone be in this country and *not* fall in love with it?

"Now, the Highland games are practiced all over the world. But"—Finn leans in, like he's about to tell a secret—"I think we can all agree that no one does it like East Lothian."

He ends his speech by saying something in Scots Gaelic that gets the crowd cheering. I can't help but get caught up in the excitement. I whistle and holler along with everyone else. Today is going to be a great day.

"Oh good," Beatrice says, clapping her hands together. "The gang's all here."

"Where?" I ask Beatrice, searching for Callum, Mhairi, and Bethany. She points to a group of boys I've never seen in my entire life. They approach us and greet Beatrice with cheek-kisses and Penelope with hugs. Then Finn jogs over from the stage and claps them all on the back. I'm left standing outside the circle, feeling incredibly awkward and regretting my commitment to spending the whole day with them.

"Everyone, everyone," Finn says as the hellos die down. "I'd like you all to meet American Hannah. She's working at the castle this summer."

I know the words he said are essentially true. And I know he can't very well say *This is Hannah, the girl I orgasmed with last night* to his friends, but I feel so random, so overlooked in this moment. So out of place. Beatrice, however, belongs. She's so poised, she's taking charge of the introductions—as though I'm her guest, not Finn's.

"Hannah," she says, presenting a tall, lanky guy with blond curls. "This is Hugo. He and Finn were at Eton together."

"A pleasure to meet you, American Hannah." Hugo shakes my hand and grins at me. I like him immediately.

"And this," Beatrice says, moving on to a handsome South Asian guy, "is Albie. Finn's friend from uni."

"All right there, Hannah? I hope Scotland's been treating you well."

Beatrice moves through the introduction of several more boys, all wonderfully kind and welcoming. Finn's in the mix of this group, but he keeps stealing glances at me and I can't tell what he's thinking. Is he happy I'm here or am I getting in the way?

We're directed by security to a VIP area where we watch the strongest locals do the caber toss. I assumed the winner is whoever throws it the farthest, but Albie explains to me that they're trying to do something much more specific.

"There's a clock on the field and the point is for the log to land in the twelve o'clock position."

"When I think logs, I think firewood," I tell him. "That thing he's throwing is a full-blown *tree.*"

"You're both wrong, it's a caber," Hugo says.

Finn approaches and claps Hugo on the back. "This lad is one-quarter Scottish and thinks that makes him an expert, but he's never even had the guts to try haggis."

"Please don't use the word 'guts,'" Hugo replies.

"I'll try it," I say. I draw the line at blood sausage, but I should try at least one local delicacy. "It's got to be good if it's still this popular."

"Really? You'll give it a go?" Finn ensures I'm serious. When I shrug my shoulders like eating it would be no big deal, he declares, "Haggis for everyone."

While they're setting up for the hammer throw, we each get a plate of haggis and gravy from the booth we saw when we arrived. Before we try it, Finn leans in and whispers, "I'll remind you that if a single one of you makes a face or spits this out, the paps will catch it on film, and you'll essentially have started a war between Scotland and England."

"He's joking, of course," Penelope says. "He's also very much not joking."

"All smiles, everyone," Beatrice says, lifting a fork.

I take a bite along with everyone else. As far as I'm concerned, the warning wasn't necessary. I'll eat pretty much anything if it comes with gravy. If any of the other haggis-eaters aren't impressed, they don't let on.

"You're all officially Scottish now," Hugo says, in his best brogue.

"The quarter Scot declares it, so it must be so," I say, earning a laugh from the group.

We watch the hammer throw, something called weight for height (a bunch of beefy people chuck a fifty-six-pound weight over what looks like a high jump bar), and the stone put. In between, we try every food the vendors offer: steak-and-cheese handheld pies, warm pretzels, ice cream. Before the crowds disperse, we're ushered to the cars by security. I somehow end up in Hugo's car with Penelope and Albie. I don't know who's riding with Finn, but I'm sure Beatrice must be in there.

While Hugo's driving to the beach, Albie turns around to address Penelope and me.

"So give us the tea, then," he says. "Is our man Finneas back with Bea?"

I will myself not to react by looking out the window at the sea.

"Come on, Pops," Hugo chimes in. "Tell us about your brother. He was so gutted when she dumped him the first time, has he really gone back for seconds?"

"Why is it," Penelope says, "that every time I get stuck with you lot, you try to gossip with me like old hens? Haven't you got your own lives?"

Hugo and Albie exchange a look. Then Albie turns directly to me.

"American Hannah," he coos. "You've wormed your way into Finn's cold heart and befriended him during his time of need. What can you tell us about Bea showing up even though they've broken up?"

I give him a beatific smile despite the way my stomach is twisting—and it isn't from the haggis. "You know as much as I do, Albie."

We get to the beach and it's completely empty, even though it's a beautiful night that promises unobstructed views of the northern lights. *This is how he moves through life,* I think. *Security clears the way so he can pretend he's just like everyone else.* We get out of the cars, and I see what look like three-wheeled makeshift go-carts with bright sails attached.

"We have one more game to enjoy while we have the remnants of daylight," Finn shouts, and the group whoops. "It's time for our annual land-yachting regatta. Pick your partner, everyone. Remember to choose wisely."

Albie snags Penelope as a partner, and she seems too pleased by the partnership, I wonder if when she gets older something could develop there. I've seen her watching him throughout the day. I assume Beatrice and Finn will partner up, so I scan the crowd for Hugo, the only other person I've really gotten to know so far. But Finn catches my arm.

"I think it's only fair," he says, loudly enough for everyone else to hear, "that the winner of last year's regatta gets stuck with the newbie."

"Oh, thanks so much," I say sarcastically. He gives me a secret wink. I wish I could read his mind. Albie's questions about Beatrice are prodding me. I wish I could know whether spending this time with her is reigniting old feelings and I'm nothing more than a rebound for him.

Or maybe I don't wish I could read his mind at all. I'm not sure I want to know the answers to these questions.

"Do you want to drive or push?" he asks me.

"Drive," I say, having no idea what we're about to do.

Each team gathers at the starting line. The finish line is down the beach, indicated by a Scottish flag.

"That's good luck for me," Hugo declares. Everyone boos him.

Finn leans down to give me pointers about steering. I'm barely listening. This is the closest his face has been to mine all day, and I want to kiss him, to feel his cheek against mine. I want the low voice he uses when he's turned on. I want to know that I'm the one he wants, not Beatrice. He finishes his speech. I haven't heard a word.

"Ready?" he asks.

"*So* ready," I fib. I grab his kilt to bring him back to me. "Wait. Has anyone ever died in a land-yachting accident?"

He laughs and puts a helmet on me. When it's buckled, he gently chucks me under my chin with his knuckle.

Rather than participate, Beatrice is at the finish line to judge the winner. The wind kicks up and the participants cheer. Apparently, the wind is a good thing even though I'm envisioning my land yacht being swept up by it and carried into the ocean. I look at my sail, noting all the extra lines and ropes, and realize this contraption is way more complicated than I thought. Getting distracted while Finn was telling me what to do was a mistake.

A whistle blows and chaos ensues. Partners shove land yachts while drivers steer into (or out of, I have no idea what I'm doing) the wind. Finn is shouting directions at me as he pushes me. Everyone else is so far ahead, their partners running after them, while I . . . tip over into the sand. Finn is laughing so hard he falls over too. He unbuckles my helmet, and I climb out of the yacht just as the sail falls on top of us. We laugh harder.

"Well, at least we're alone," Finn says, making no move to take the sail off us since it's blocking us from everyone else down the beach.

It's our first moment of real privacy all day and I simply can't help myself.

"Your friends were asking Penelope about you and Beatrice, since she's back in your life, and I know we talked about this last night and I'm sorry I'm asking again, but I have to know: Is being around her this much going to make you fall for her again?" I blurt out. "It's okay if the answer's yes—I mean, it's not okay, but I'd rather know now."

We're lying on the sand, our faces so close I can feel his breath on me. I can't see anything except the yellows and whites of the sail, like a stained glass window.

"No, of course not," he says. He tilts my chin so I can look at him. "I thought I've made it clear that I only want you."

"But doesn't she make more sense for you?" I protest, not because I want it to be true, but because I'm scared it is. And as much as I don't want to think about Tina's warning to me, it's been creeping into my thoughts all day. "Am I just getting in the way of what's best for you?"

"Hannah, listen to me," he says softly. "Yes, Beatrice and I make sense on paper. But she only sees the person I have to be for the public, for my parents. I appreciate her for that, of course there's value in the way she understands my day-to-day life. But she doesn't understand the day-to-day *me* the way you do. You see me for who I am. Always."

"But—"

"My god, you're a pain in my royal arse," he continues, throwing his head back as much as this position we're in will allow. "But you also make me laugh and turn me on, so please stop trying to set me up with my ex-girlfriend just so you never have to land-sail again."

This gets a laugh out of me. In addition to feeling better about Beatrice because I believe every word he says, I feel myself falling for him faster. Deeper.

In the distance, we hear the cheers of a winner and the heckles of several losers. But all that disappears when Finn leans in to kiss me. It's tender, the way his lips brush against mine as he cups my jaw with his hand. I open my mouth and move as closely to him as I can get underneath this land yacht. We're going to have sand all through our clothes and hair, but I don't care.

Nor do I care that through the white of the sail, I catch hints of the greens of the aurora borealis. I'm missing it. But nothing, not even the northern lights, can compare to what I feel with Finn.

21

"What in the* Bridgerton *is this email?" I ask, flipping my phone around to show Caro. We're back in the gift shop today because the royal family, Finn included, is in Glasgow. Inveresk Castle and our gift shop are open to the public while they're away.

"*That,*" Caro says, tapping the phone screen, "is a reminder about the Ghillies Ball." I look at her blankly and she grabs my arm dramatically. *"Hannah!"*

"What?" I'm so confused and incredibly tired from the late night at the beach, my reading-comprehension skills are that of a snail. "Can you explain this email to me like I'm five?"

"Late night with a certain prince?" she asks, waggling her eyebrows at me.

"And his ex-girlfriend," I point out. I haven't told Caro much of anything about the time I've spent with Finn. She knows the bare minimum (and the PG version, at that). I want to tell her everything, I really do.

But.

I know what it's like to trust someone and have them throw that trust back in my face. People can surprise you in good ways and bad. Besides, talking to Caro, a person who works at the castle and knows everyone else who works here, about my relationship with Finn is just about as risky as it gets. All it would take is one slipup for this to become front-page news. Literally.

Thankfully, pointing out Beatrice's presence at the castle is enough for Caro to stop teasing me about my feelings for Finn. She grabs one of the coffee-table books about Inveresk Castle off the display shelf and flips through it until she finds the page on the Ghillies Ball. Cracking the book wide, Caro puts it on the counter for me to look at.

"The Ghillies Ball is an annual tradition started by Queen Victoria and her husband, Prince Albert," she tells me, pointing to an artist's rendering of one of the earliest examples of the celebration.

"Wait—why was Victoria called the queen, and her husband referred to as a prince?" I squint at the picture and reach for the travel mug of instant coffee mixed with hot chocolate I brought in with me today. "Doesn't that make it sound like she married her son?"

"Don't be daft," Caro says, rolling her eyes at me. "If people around here knew how little you know about the royals . . ."

I'm actually quite intimately acquainted with them, I think, smiling into my mug.

"What are you cheesing about?" Caro gives me a hip-check.

"I just think your accent is cute," I tell Caro and give her a hip-check back. "Now, tell me about this ball—and promise me we can get ready for it together."

"You're the one with the accent here," she reminds me. "And you bet. I'd love to get all gussied up with you! Okay, so. Back to your Scottish history lesson. Queen Victoria purchased this castle in 1852. In the summer, she threw a party to thank her staff for all their hard work. It's been an annual tradition ever since then."

Caro explains to me that "ghillie" is Gaelic for gamekeeper, but Ghillies are also what the Highland dancers I saw wore on their feet.

"It's dead brilliant," she says. "The staff get all dressed up and party it up with the royal family, and for one night, we're all the same. It's my single favorite day of the year. Oh! We should go into town tomorrow after work and shop for dresses together."

"Yes, I'd love that," I tell her, already imagining myself slow-dancing with Finn in a ballroom.

"Good morning, lasses," Beverly says, entering the store. "How are we faring today?"

"I'm just telling Hannah here about Ghillies," Caro tells her.

"Ghillies," Beverly responds, beaming. "My favorite day of the year."

"Duffie and I are going to give you and Ethel a run for your money for cutest couple this year," Caro declares.

I beam at Beverly. "You and Ethel are together? I had no idea. I *love* her."

"So do I," Beverly says with a wink. "Even if she'll one day be the death of me with her nagging about my getting in her way in the kitchen."

While Caro and Beverly relive some Ghillies and gowns from the past, I let my mind wander again to the ball. I picture myself leaving the party, arm in arm with Finn, making him laugh, having him lean down to kiss me—being a couple out in the open. My thoughts are interrupted by two adorable new customers.

"Eileen! Bill!" I exclaim. When my temporary landlords promised to visit me, I wasn't sure they really meant it. I introduce them to Caro and Beverly, who talk me up.

"She's lighting up the place, and selling all sorts of trinkets," Beverly says.

"Good on ya, lass," Bill says to me with a wink.

"It's been an age since we've been here," Eileen says, looking around the store.

"Souvenirs have certainly changed since then," Bill agrees, picking up one of the Finn bobbleheads.

"Are you in the market for something today?" I ask them, still unable to believe they came to see me. "Or just having a look around? Hey, how's the pub doing?"

"It's as busy as ever," Bill tells me, shaking his head in

wonder. He leans in conspiratorially. "I wouldn't mind getting a wee gift for Eileen. Surprise her, eh?"

"I'm on it," I tell him, and shoot Caro a text to distract Eileen while Bill and I shop. Caro starts telling Eileen about Ghillies, taking her full attention, while Bill manages to purchase her a pair of lovely floral slippers, patterned after the gardens here. I give Bill a fist bump and we share a conspiratorial chuckle as he tucks the tissue-wrapped slippers into his bag.

"Don't be a stranger, bonny," Eileen says. "We love to see how you're getting on."

"Aye, come to the pub and we'll treat you to a pie and a pint," Bill adds.

"I'll visit as soon as I can," I promise, walking them out.

"They're a right cute couple," Caro muses once they're gone. "I hope Duffie and I grow up to be like them."

"Couple goals for sure," I agree.

When she and Beverly go back to talking about Ghillies, I think about Eileen and Bill and wanting what they have too, but a shadow is hanging over my head. The image of Finn and me dancing at the ball . . . how realistic is it? At what point will he tell his family about us? When can we stop hiding and start being Bill and Eileen, or Caro and Duffie, or Ethel and Beverly?

The prospect of Ghillies, the point of which is to celebrate the staff and make us all equals for a night, is starting to remind me how impossible my feelings for Prince Finneas are.

It's taken time and more research than I expected, but I'm finally hitting my stride with my book. After work, I sit down at the kitchen table in my cottage and start typing. I'm so lost in the world of my story I don't even realize how long I've been at it until there's a tap at the back window of my cottage.

I try to temper my hopes, knowing Finn's in Glasgow with his family, but when I peek through the lace curtain, my hopes turn into pure excitement. I slip on my shoes and run out the front door and around the cottage to meet him in the back. Before he can even say hello, I throw my arms around him.

"I've missed you too," he says, resting his cheek on my hair. "My pocket-sized American pinup girl."

"My parents call me 'Tinkerbell,' you know," I say, as we pull away to grin at each other like fools. "Because I'm so short."

He holds my hands. "Do you miss them?"

"Yes and no. Hey, how was Glasgow?"

He winces comically. "Did you just call it 'Glass-gow'? My darling, it's 'Glas-go.' You're not only making up words, you're making up pronunciations now. Not even Shakespeare did that."

I try to scowl at him, but his use of "darling" has turned my insides into goo.

"Speaking of the bard," he says. "Grab your coat and your purse. I'm taking you on a date."

"What does this date have to do with Shakespeare?" I ask, walking back around the cottage to get my things. Once inside, I save my document and freshen up my makeup. I debate changing into something more date-ish. Quickly, I throw on a casual dress, a cardigan, and my pink Chucks, and pull my hair out of its braid. It's wavy, falling around my face in a thankfully flattering way. Yanking out a braid can go either way. I lock my cottage door behind me and join him in the back.

He eyes me appreciatively. "I've a mind to cancel this spectacular evening I've planned for us and just snog you all night in the woods instead."

"Either one works for me." I take his hand. He squeezes it and leads me down the road where a sleek black car is parked.

As he drives us toward Edinburgh, he talks to me about his day. Instead of the business aspects of the trip to Glasgow, he explains some of his complicated family dynamics, and I learn to read him better: The corners of his eyes crinkle as he tells me that Poppy kept gushing about how much she loved spending time with me yesterday. His brows lower when he mentions the pressure his dad is putting on him to be more involved with the family, even though he basically exiled Finn this summer.

"He can't have it both ways," Finn says, his jaw flexing in consternation. "You can't say 'Be more involved with the family' and then bugger off to the South of France, leaving me behind."

"I'm sorry. That's completely unfair to you. I get that there's this immense pressure on all of you to keep up appearances, but you're also a twenty-year-old who got his heart broken and wanted to make some bad decisions to get over it. You should be allowed to do that without the commonwealth falling apart at your antics."

Finn exhales, a wry smile slowly stretching across his face. "I feel like a top-tier asshat whenever I complain about my life, considering the privilege that comes with all this."

"Both things can be true. You can be a top-tier asshat *and* deserve compassion."

Finn starts to say something and stops himself.

"What is it? You can tell me anything."

"When I asked you if you missed your parents, you said yes *and* no. I don't want to pry, but if you want to talk about that . . ."

I never talk about my relationship with my parents. Not with them, not even with Gigi or Dean. But Finn has just opened up to me, and I trust him with my most vulnerable thoughts in a way I've never trusted anyone else.

"I feel like a horrible person admitting this, but it's actually a relief to be away from them." I look out the window at the Scottish countryside, the green fading as dusk settles over the hills. "I love them, but it's hard to focus on my own life, to process the good and the bad things that happen to me, when they're always dragging me into their dysfunctional relationship."

"Two things can be true," he says, echoing my words. "You can be relieved to be away from your parents *and* be a good person."

"Your response was much nicer than my response."

"You may be a 'good' person, but I'm a *really* good person," he says solemnly. I playfully pinch his arm.

Finn turns down a country road, a few miles away from Edinburgh. Part of me, the part that always expects a plan and direction, wants to ask again where we're going. Instead, I settle into the not knowing. After all, he clearly wants to surprise me. We make another turn and pull into a lot. There's a helicopter in front of us.

"Um, Finn?" I say, my head spinning.

"Yes, American Hannah?"

"Are we getting on that thing?"

"Much to the chagrin of my security detail, we are." He parks the car, opens the door for me, and leads me to the helipad.

Getting into the helicopter is not something I manage with grace, considering how fitted my dress is around my hips and thighs. My foot slips and Finn "helps" by pushing on my ass. Well, "pushing" is generous—he's mostly just squeezing it, which makes me laugh and slip again. We put on our seat belts and headsets, the propeller whirls powerfully, and soon the chopper tilts to one side and the other as it lifts into the air. I let out a string of curse words.

"Hannah," he chides, clutching invisible pearls. "I can't believe you kiss me with that mouth."

Helicopter pilot be damned, I lean over and kiss him right then and there. Being with him is joy. Pure, silly, wonderful joy.

Even though I could happily spend the helicopter ride making out with Finn, I don't want to miss this once-in-a-lifetime view. And looking out the window of an airplane is nothing compared to this. We fly over Edinburgh. I immediately spot Holyrood Palace and Edinburgh Castle, which orients me well enough to point out The High Road Pub, where we met. Neither of us has to say anything. He simply squeezes my thigh as we fly over it.

He points out stadiums I immediately forget the names of. We head south over the cityscape, green pastures, and gorgeous lakes. I'm taking in so much beauty all at once, I'm no longer talking, just shaking Finn and pointing. But when I look back to make sure he's seeing what I'm seeing, he's looking at me.

"What's that?" I ask, pointing to a new city.

"Manchester, darling."

"Is that where we're going?" I ask, my stomach fluttering again at the term of endearment.

He shrugs. We pass over Manchester and soon the helicopter lowers.

"I have no idea where I am," I tell Finn, taking my headset off, "but wherever it is, I love it."

"Getting you in the helicopter was such a chore, I just hope you're able to get out and see it," Finn teases, kissing my nose.

"How about if I just fling myself out of the helicopter and you catch me."

"My security detail can only take so much, Hannah."

I do manage to get out of the chopper without too much trouble. Dark clouds are slowly moving in, but I don't care. I'm already having the best night of my life.

A very solemn-looking chauffeur in a dark suit ushers us into the back seat of a sleek car, then drives off. I press my face to the window, searching for some indication of where we are. And then I see the sign.

Stratford-upon-Avon.

"You brought me to Shakespeare's birthplace?" I say, *ooh*ing at the quaint little town as it comes into view. It looks like something out of a storybook.

"I figure since you're a wordsmith just as he was, it'd be a good fit." He takes my hand. "Who knows, perhaps Shakespeare's ghost will appear and tell you what you and I already know: You're a writer."

He's obviously teasing me about the "swoonable" moment, but he's also telling me he has faith in my lofty writing-career goals. In me. Unexpected emotion forms in my chest and rises up my throat. This surprise date has already been over-the-top. Yet, when I look at Finn, I don't see a prince. I see a boy who is very much trying to tell a girl how much he cares for her. The words I want to say to him are too heavy, too soon. I tell him another truth instead. "This is perfect. *You* are perfect." I kiss him, despite the driver a few feet away, because I need him to know. He and the helicopter pilot can exchange notes later, for all I care.

The car pulls over and stops. The driver looks at us through the rearview mirror.

"A respectful reminder to stay to the route and locations that have been approved, Your Highness," he says.

"Of course." Finn unbuckles his seat belt. "Thank you, Mason."

We get out of the car, and I drink this new magical place in. To our left is a charming little arched bridge over a canal lined with colorful boats. To our right is a line of shops, some Tudor-style, some red brick. He takes my hand, and we start walking toward the shops.

"This is the best day of my life," I tell him. "Tell all the guys of my future to pack it in, because you'll never be outdone."

His brow furrows and he's about to say something that seems as though it might be important, when his attention darts behind me.

"Shit," he mutters. He pulls on the handle of the nearest shop and ushers me inside.

"Everything okay?" I ask, shuffling inside what turns out to be a secondhand bookshop.

"Of course," he says, but he's still eyeing the glass panel of the door. He puts a hand on the small of my back and leads me farther into the store.

"Let me know if I can help you," an elderly bespectacled man at the counter says without looking up from his own book.

We're in the back of the store now, in the mystery/thriller section. "Why are we in here? What happened out there?"

"There was someone outside by the bridge who saw us and immediately pulled out their phone." Finn sighs and looks up at the ceiling. "I wanted to get us away before they took our photo."

His explanation doesn't sit right with me. Yes, there was a time when I didn't want to be photographed with him—worried about what professors and other students might think of me in the fall. That's changed now. I'm proud to be at his side. I *want* people to know how I feel about him.

"There were photographers everywhere at the Highland games," I point out.

"That was different," he says quietly.

I want to ask how, but I already know how. Beatrice was at his side during those shots. I was off to the side in my discount dress and pink Chucks.

My stomach drops. Insecurity splashes down on me

fiercely and I can't stop the words from coming out. "Are you ashamed of me?"

Finn looks genuinely surprised. "What?"

"Are you ashamed to be seen with me? With *just* me?" My voice wavers slightly. I manage to stand my ground, to keep eye contact while I wait for the truth. "I get it. I mean, I'm a clumsy American who can barely get in and out of a helicopter, so—"

"Hannah." Finn brings both his hands to my cheeks and leans down until our foreheads touch. "I wasn't protecting me, I was protecting *you.* I don't have a choice about being in the media. I was born into it. But you? I don't want them treating you badly. Saying ugly things just to get a rise out of us."

"Okay." I think I believe him. I want to.

Finn must sense my hesitation. He brushes my hair away from my face. "Why would I ever be ashamed of you? You are perfect."

A sweet heat licks at my cheeks. I cover up my bashfulness with a joke. "You're right. I am perfect. You, on the other hand . . . What am I going to do with you?" I lift onto my tiptoes and kiss him until we bump into a bookshelf, and we both start quietly snickering. And then I kiss him some more.

22

Standing in front of the cottage where Shakespeare's wife, Anne Hathaway, once lived, with its thatched roof and sweet garden, gives me chills. Hesitantly, I reach out and place my hand on one of the exterior wood beams, rubbed smooth by the centuries. Could he have once touched this same spot? This is where Anne lived before they married, and I can imagine the young bard standing outside the cottage, fidgeting nervously, as he mustered up the courage to visit the older woman who'd stolen his heart.

"Shall we go in?" Finn asks.

"I think it's closed," I say, pointing at the clearly marked sign. Finn gives me a look. "Oh, right." Of course. We took a helicopter here, for goodness' sake. Obviously Finn planned on pulling some strings. He pushes the door open, and, once again, I wonder if Shakespeare ever heard that exact squeak.

The house is empty. I imagine Finn's handlers arranged for the night staff to lie low.

His security detail also does a very good job of remaining in the periphery. It reminds me of something I heard about security at Disneyland: You can't always see them, but trust that they're there and they mean business.

Because the ceiling is so low, Finn has to stoop in places as we walk through the cottage.

"Finally, a home that's my size," I say as he avoids hitting his head on the doorway.

"It's perfect for a Tinkerbell," he agrees.

The house is beautifully preserved. There are dark wooden beams running along the white ceiling; the stone floors are sturdy and clean. I can picture Snow White sweeping up in here.

"Historians have been unfair to Anne," Finn says. "She and Shakespeare married when she was pregnant, she was several years older than he was, and therefore she's been depicted as a calculating shrew."

"Imagine not knowing much about a woman and immediately assuming the worst," I say dryly. "Thankfully, society doesn't do *that* anymore."

We duck into a chamber. I point at the bed, which is the size of a twin. "They had to have a good relationship if that's the bed they shared."

"I'm not sure they would've both slept here," Finn says. "I have to check the timeline."

"Do you have to be so literal? Just let me imagine the greatest English writer in history doing it in this room."

"*Doing it?* I knew you were American. I didn't know you'd teleported here from 1980s America."

We sit on a wooden bench outside, even though the sky is continuing to darken and there's a solid chance we'll be rained on. Still, I don't want this part of our date to end yet. I inhale deeply, wondering which of these plants would've bloomed in Shakespeare's day. Which might've made their way into his work.

"'I know a bank where the wild thyme blows. . . .'" I begin.

"'Where oxlips and the nodding violet grows.'" Finn grins. "You know Oberon's famous speech."

"*A Midsummer Night's Dream* is one of my favorites."

"Did you have to memorize the passage for school?"

"Um, no." I scoff. "I think that's more of an Eton thing."

"So how do you know it?"

I shrug. "I've just read it a bunch."

"You're really one of the most passionate people I've ever met, American Hannah. You do things because you *want* to. Not because they're expected of you."

"Maybe . . . in some ways. So what are you passionate about?"

"Besides you?" he says cheekily.

"Besides me. If you didn't have all your family obligations, what life would you be pursuing? What sort of career would you want to have?"

Finn grows thoughtful as the wind picks up, swirling our hair like cotton candy. "If I could do whatever I wanted, I would've studied medicine. My family members are patrons and presidents of various hospitals, but I always feel several steps removed from the actual 'helping' part. Certainly, we attract attention and money for the organizations. It's not the same as treating the patients, though, is it?"

His confession reminds me of the day he found me crying in the alleyway behind the pub, when I was sure I'd have to fly home. I never understood why he was so motivated to help me and chalked it up to an attraction. I see now it was more than that. Finn feels at his best when he can help someone in a concrete way.

"You would've been a great doctor," I tell him, and rest my head on his shoulder.

We're quiet. I'm imagining a life with him. Us, living in an apartment; me writing novels while he goes through medical school. An ache, a longing, for something we can't ever have brews deep within me.

Our driver, Mason, enters the back garden, looking distressed. "Your Highness, I'm afraid the helicopter will be unable to fly you back to Inveresk tonight."

A storm we've barely noticed is rumbling around us. I've seen the stories on the news about helicopter accidents, and, even though I'm concerned about my shift at the gift shop tomorrow, I'm definitely not interested in getting in a death trap.

"Do we have a plan, then?" Finn asks.

Mason nods. "We've arranged for you two to stay at a hotel in the city center. The room is under my name—number 305. I'll give you the key card so you can enter through the back without being seen by staff."

A night in a hotel room. With Finn. If I so much as look at him, I know I'll blush.

"Thank you, Mason. We appreciate it." Finn's voice sounds strained—and not in a bad way. He also must be thinking about what the privacy of this hotel room means.

Mason drives us to Stratford's high street, then takes us around an alleyway and indicates the door our key will allow us to enter through. He takes off his suit jacket so that Finn can hold it above our heads as we run through the rain. It's a warm summer storm. My arms and legs are covered in goose bumps that have nothing to do with the weather.

The hotel is an elegant stone building. Inside, the lighting is low and sexy; there are sconces on the walls and antique iron-and-rope chandeliers overhead. We walk down a hall lined in restored wooden wainscot until we reach our room, which is up a small flight of stairs and tucked away in a corner. When Mason promised us discretion, he delivered.

Finn swallows hard and opens the door to the room. The walls are all burgundy with dark wood beams; in the corner, under ornate, black-and-white window treatments, are two modern wingback chairs and an antique-looking table. Almost immediately, our combined attention goes to the plush king-sized bed with a silk canopy overtop.

"Did you plan all this to get me into bed?" I ask.

"You mean, did I summon the storm? I know the American education system leaves something to be desired, but surely you know that humans can't control the weather."

"Royals can," I tease. "There was a whole thread about it on Reddit."

"What's Reddit?"

I snort. "Are you serious?" He nods. "It's a site with all these discussion topics. . . . You know what, never mind. Thinking about internet nerds is kinda ruining the vibe."

"Well, now, I am sorry about that." He wraps an arm around my waist and pulls me to him. "Let's see what we can do about getting something else on your mind," he says, before leaning down and pressing his lips to mine.

My back arches in response. My mouth opens so our tongues can meet and explore. As the kiss deepens, so does the warm, exquisite feeling of want pooling deep in my belly. I lift a knee, which he catches by running his hand down my back to my thigh. He holds my leg up and presses himself into me. I whimper into his mouth.

"Oh, the things I want to do to you in this room. In this bed," he says, walking us back toward the mattress. "But if you want to stop at any time—"

"Yes, same, same," I say, greedily touching him.

I'm so turned on, I want him—*all* of him—so badly, I can't even make another joke about the canopy. Our clothes are damp from the rain, so I begin unbuttoning his shirt, kissing him as he falls back onto the bed. I climb on top of him and start moving my hips. His eyes close as his chest rises and falls in ecstasy. He hasn't seen anything yet. This hotel room is an opportunity we may not have again, and I'm determined to make the most of being tucked away in this little town where no one (save for his zipped-lips security team) can find us. Especially since I already got a preview of how things will be between us the night Finn snuck into my cottage back at the castle.

I lift my body off him to give him room to undo his belt and unbutton his pants. I climb down from the bed to slip his pants off the rest of the way.

"Can I—?" I ask. He nods. I rub my palms up his legs and over his briefs. Tonight, I'm going to have *all of him.* Slowly, so slowly, I pull his briefs off.

"*Hannah*," he moans. "You'll be the death of me."

I smile and drink in his naked body: the defined muscles of his shoulders and arms, his sculpted chest and abdomen . . . all of him is beautiful.

However, I'm still very much clothed. It's nothing I've ever done before with Dean, but I decide to turn undressing into a bit of a show. Being with Finn makes me brave. He makes me feel safe with my vulnerability. This is a guy who gave me a new job in a new place, who helped me get out of my head and enjoy the pleasure he can offer me. Tonight, I'm ready to do something else new with him.

Leaving my dress where it is, I reach underneath and pull down the lace underwear I have on. The instant I step out of it, his head drops onto the bed, and he moans again. I smile and clear my throat, reminding him my performance isn't over. He sits up, his weight held by his arms. His hazel eyes, which look like liquid gold, run over the length of me.

"More," he commands.

Since the bodice of my dress is fitted enough that I didn't need to put on a bra, the second I unzip it, I'll be naked, and where's the fun of not teasing him a little more? I take off one earring and another while he drops his head in agony. As soon as his chin lifts, I reach behind me to methodically unzip the dress. Before it can fall to my waist, I turn around so he can only see my bare back and cheekily look over my shoulder. I never imagined feeling this safe with a partner. This free to explore my sexuality and let him slowly take in my body.

Everything with Finn is different than I'm used to. Everything is better.

"*More*," he says again.

The dress drops to the floor, giving him full view of my ass. He lets out an appreciative breath. I turn, feeling every bit the sexy pinup girl he accused me of resembling the first night we met, and stand before him, fully naked. His eyes take in their fill.

"I'm going to need you to come over to this bed immediately." The commanding tone of his voice is so seductive, but I use every ounce of willpower to cross the room slowly. He's sitting up now, his arms outstretched to receive me. When I'm close enough, he buries his face in my breasts; he runs his hands up my legs to cup my bottom. I've never felt this attractive, this *worshipped.*

"When you told me back at Anne Hathaway's garden you were sorry that I never got to choose things for myself," he says into my skin.

"Yeah?" I'm breathing hard.

"You were wrong." He lifts his head. "I do get to choose sometimes. And I choose you."

Taking his jaw in one hand, I reward him with a heated kiss. His hands continue to explore my body, to run delicately, playfully, over my skin. I climb up onto the bed, onto Finn. The intimate contact makes us hum in pleasure into each other's mouths. But it's time. Foreplay is no longer on the menu: I need friction, I need us to move together, I need . . .

"More," I say, pressing kisses along his jawline. "Please tell me you have a condom."

"I came prepared," he replies. "Hopeful."

We stop long enough for him to slip off the bed and get a condom out of the pocket of his trousers. He rolls it on and checks in with me before he comes back to the bed. I nod, *Yes.* As he fills me, something more than pleasure ripples through my core. It's belonging. We belong to each other, Finn and me.

We move together; he touches me until I cry out, riding the most exquisite climax of my life. His body collapses on top of mine. I hold him to me as long as I dare. I'm on the pill too, so I'm not that concerned. I want to lie like this with him forever.

After a moment, he rolls over. When our eyes meet, his expression must mirror mine because what I'm feeling, what I'm seeing, is love.

This could really be something. Us. Together.

23

It isn't simply the fact that I don't have anything in my wardrobe—washed or piling up in my laundry bin—that screams "ball at a Scottish castle." It isn't just that I'm still recovering from my impromptu night in Stratford-upon-Avon, even though that was days ago. There's a strange tension in the air. Caro's been in my cottage for a whole minute, and she hasn't said a word. By now, she should've told me at least eight different stories and I should've had to ask her to translate a bevy of words.

"Is it okay if I put my stuff down on your bed?" she asks. She's holding a garment bag and smaller bag, presumably full of hair accessories and makeup.

"Of course." I walk over to my wardrobe, willing one of my casual summer dresses I got on sale at H&M to turn into something ball-worthy. "Please tell me I won't be the only one there without something appropriate to wear."

Caro shrugs noncommittally.

"Caro?" Her iciness has been going on for days. Ever since I missed that shopping trip we'd planned because I was secretly with Finn in another country, we've barely talked. When things weren't busy at the shop, she'd claim she had to do inventory in the back or run an errand for Beverly.

Caro puts her stuff on my bed, sighs, and turns to look at me. "Hannah?"

"Are we fighting?" I ask.

"How would I know?" she asks. "I barely know anything about you."

"What are you talking about?" It's not unusual for me to struggle to follow Caro's fast talking, but this time I understood her, and I still have no idea what she's saying.

"Where were you the day you called in sick for work and said you couldn't go shopping with me?"

"I . . ." Lying about being sick when I was next to Finn in our secret little hotel room was different than lying to her face. I can't do it.

"Aye, that's what I thought." Caro furiously turns her back to me and begins unpacking her accessories. "I'm not a fool, even though you treat me like one. You're not the only one who was missing that day. People were talking about it."

My body turns cold, despite the muggy, summer heat in this cottage. Inveresk Castle is like its own little community; people notice things. Like Caro said, people talk.

Caro gives up on her accessories and flops down onto my bed. "I really thought we were friends, Hannah. After everything I've told you about me and Duffie, I thought you might open up to me too. Instead, you've said nothing. Nothing about your life back in America, nothing about what's clearly going on here. You told me you and Finn kissed ages ago and then never mentioned him again. It's like you don't trust me."

My mind is racing through images of Finn and Gigi and Dean and my parents and Beatrice and the royal family and back to Finn. I nearly tell her I barely trust anyone anymore. But then I'd have to tell her why.

My hesitancy to refute her claim has gone on for too long, and Caro mumbles, "Never mind. Maybe I should go."

"Don't go." The request comes out soft and quiet, but it's sincere. I sit down on the bed next to her. "You know I came to Scotland for the job with Margaret MacIntyre that didn't pan out. I came for another reason too."

Normally, Caro would insert a joke here or tease me to get me to say more. Instead, she's silent. It's a side of her I haven't experienced all summer, and I'm starting to understand the depth of her hurt. Caro hasn't done anything to me except be my friend and try to get to know me. I'm the problem here. It's time for me to make it right. To start with the truth about why I'm at Inveresk Castle.

I play with a loose thread on my shorts. "There was an additional piece of motivation to get out of the US for a while."

I take a shuddery breath because apparently I'm not

done crying about Gigi yet. I wonder if I ever will be. I tell Caro everything: how I found out she and Dean were sneaking around behind my back, how I confronted them; the fact that the person I thought would be my best friend for life is someone I don't speak to anymore. Caro listens. Ever empathetic, her face reflects my own emotions. And then she tells me about the time she discovered her mom's boyfriend was cheating and how she was the one to break the news. How awful it was. Throughout the conversation, the ice between us gets chipped away. But when we get to the end, there's still hurt in her eyes.

"Caro, I—" A knock at the door interrupts my apology. I open it and see a young man I vaguely recognize as the porter who helped me with my luggage the first day I arrived at the castle. He's holding a large, flat white box with a white silk ribbon.

"For you," he says.

I thank him and take it. When I turn around, Caro is staring suspiciously at both me and this box.

"What is that?" she asks.

I shrug. My hands are shaking, my mind jumbled. I truly don't know what's in this box, but chances are it's a gift from Finn. Choosing to open it in front of Caro is risky—and another step in the right direction. Trusting her with my past that exists in another country wasn't hard and I want to trust her with this too.

I set the box down and blurt out, "I had sex with Finn."

Caro's responding laugh is a full-bellied cackle. She falls onto the bed. Through wheezes, she yells, "*I knew it!*"

"No you didn't—and what do you mean?" I ask, feeling immediate relief at being able to finally talk about this monumental thing that's been happening in secret.

"Babe, you'd know if you ever actually participated in the WhatsApp group chat. Everyone's been sharing 'Finnah' sightings."

"Finnah?" I ask.

"Your portmanteau, babe. Yours and the prince's. The juiciest day of all in the group chat was the day you called in 'sick' and Finn had disappeared on 'royal business' that no one seemed to know about and wasn't in the royal calendar. And then, coincidentally, you both reappeared at the same time."

It was naive of me to think no one would clock any of the time we've been spending together. Sneaking around, as hot as it was at times, had a shelf life. And now that I know I'm falling in love with Finn, I'm craving something real with him.

The bubbles of energy created between Caro and me from my confession pop. I don't just owe her the truth, I owe her an apology.

"I'm sorry I lied to you," I say. "I'm sorry I missed our shopping date. You've been an absolute gem to me, and I've been—"

"A brick wall," Caro supplies.

"Yeah."

"I appreciate it. And that you finally told me the truth. None of that must've been easy to say." Just when the mood is growing too heavy, she suddenly shakes my shoulders dramatically and cries, "Just let me love you, for god's sake!"

I laugh and pull her in for a hug. Caro could be a friend for life if I let her. And I really want to let her. "I'm sorry again about being a brick wall."

"Ah, you've been a charming one," she says, giving me a squeeze and letting me go. "We're all rooting for you two, you know. The whole group chat."

"You are?" This comes as a surprise. Sure, the staff have all been lovely to me. Still, I assumed everyone else would see Beatrice as a much better match.

"Of course, you daft cow." We laugh and she eyes the box in my breakfast nook. "Now, if you don't open that box immediately, I'm gonna tear it open myself."

I retrieve the box so we can open it together. I pull at the silk ribbon and lift the lid. Inside is a blush-pink dress that just so happens to match my pink Chucks. *Not a coincidence,* I think.

I stand and press the gown against my body. It has a structured bodice with a sweetheart neck. Lace floral appliqués in subtle creams cascade in flattering places from the bodice down the luxurious tulle of the full skirt.

"Oh my days," Caro says, bringing her hands to her mouth.

"I know." The gown even *smells* good. I think the tissue paper it came in is scented.

"I can't believe he sent you a gown because he knew you didn't have anything to wear tonight." She clutches her heart dramatically. "That's the most romantic thing. Ever."

We finish getting ready together. There's a newfound ease and intimacy to our friendship that carries echoes of Gigi. A bittersweet feeling. Like a magician, Caro somehow arranges my blond hair into a sexy, tousled updo. She does my makeup, leaning into Hollywood glamour, and I watch in awe as she transforms her own lids into a smoky sunset that goes perfectly with her turquoise party dress.

Caro and I help each other choose a perfume for tonight and take one more look at ourselves in the bathroom mirror.

"Ready?" Caro says, adjusting a vintage pearl clip in her hair.

"Ready," I say. And I am. I'm ready for Finn. I'm ready for everything.

24

I'm so glad Caro taught me the Eightsome Reel before we came to the ball tonight. When the music kicks up and I see the circles forming, I don't hesitate to join the one that Penelope's waving me over to.

"Your pink trainers with that gown," she says, clapping her hands together. "Love, love, love."

"Thanks," I tell her. I almost mention that her brother's responsible for the dress, but I don't know how much she knows. Instead, I take in all the details of her couture gown. There's a net with appliquéd black lace covering her arms, shoulders, and clavicle. Overtop is a red tartan dress, bustled at her hip to reveal cream tulle. It's a risky look and she pulls it off. "Your gown is *killer.*"

She leans in conspiratorially as our circle begins to slowly spin. "It's Alexander McQueen and I'm obsessed. Though it caused a row with Mother already. She thinks it's too 'punk rock' for Ghillies."

"It's punk rock in the best way," I tell her before we're pulled away from each other in the course of the dance.

Our group of eight proceeds to turn and skip and hook arms. The music is lively and I'm having the best time already. The room, with its impossibly high medieval windows, is spinning around me. I dance into the center and put my hand in with everyone else's. Feeling free, I've never felt so beautiful, my blush-pink dress spinning with me. I've never felt so light on my feet or light in my heart.

As Caro told me in the shop, this ball is not only intended as a gift of gratitude, but to make staff and royals feel like equals for a night. It's succeeding. I continue dancing beside Penelope, and she keeps yelling "Dancing in these heels is daft! Give me your shoes!" while we spin and laugh. When the song ends, I'm dizzy and delighted.

I move away from the dance floor, hoping to find Finn. I've yet to see him tonight. As I make my way around the room, I pass Ethel and Beverly, arm in arm, looking regal in their beaded ensembles.

"Don't forget to hydrate," Beverly calls to me.

"And get some food on your bones," Ethel adds. "I didn't spend all day in the kitchen just so you could look at the pretty appetizers."

"I'll go eat now," I promise her and wander over to the refreshment table where Duffie and Caro are loading up plates.

"How's your first Ghillies so far?" Caro asks me.

"Amazing," I tell her, though I'm still scanning the crowd for Finn. She and I have a silent conversation.

"What are you two telepathically saying?" Duffie asks. "I know women can do that. My mum and sisters do it all the time. It's usually about me being an eejit."

Caro and I laugh. "It's not about that," she says.

"Ah, come on, Hannah. You must think I'm a right fool for not locking down Caro immediately," Duffie says sheepishly. There's an endearing little quirk to his mouth and his hair is falling over his forehead.

"Absolutely I do," I tell him, which makes Caro cackle. "I'm just glad you finally pulled your head out of your ass."

"She means 'erse,'" Caro says, giving me a wink. Then she whispers something to Duffie, likely something dirty, because he reddens and chokes on his punch. I really am rooting for those two. "We'll . . . be back."

"Go, lovebirds," I say, shooing them off.

Finn's still not here. I consider trying to get Penelope alone so I can quietly ask her where he is, if he's okay. But when she isn't with her mother, she's on the dance floor. I can't blame her. If it weren't for my growing concern, I'd be out there too.

I do another lap of the perimeter, taking in the ornate carved-wood ceiling, the crossed swords hanging high on the walls. As I'm admiring the embroidery work on the drapes, trying to determine what the shapes and symbols mean, I bump into the back of a man. For a split second, I think I've jostled Finn. But when the figure turns around, I see I'm gravely mistaken. The face may resemble Finn's, but there's nothing warm and friendly about it. This face is cold. Humorless. "I beg your pardon," King Augustus says stiffly.

As part of my training, Beverly taught me how to address the royal family. But my mind has gone completely blank. I bow my head and curtsy awkwardly. "It was my fault, Your Majesty. Your Highness. Your . . . sir."

"Ah. The American . . ."

When I have the courage to lift my gaze, his steely eyes are scrutinizing me. "I do hope you're enjoying your time in Scotland?"

"I am. I'm so grateful for the job, and for the chance to spend time on your beautiful estate."

"And I suppose access to my son was a surprise perk?"

"I'm . . . sorry, what?" I think I'm supposed to say "pardon" but I don't care.

"I'm not sure how you pulled this off. I'm rather impressed."

He knows. He knows and he's pissed. Is that why Finn isn't here? My mind is reeling. "Wait, are you saying . . . are you suggesting that this was part of some big plan? That I *tricked* him?" I can't help but laugh. "Um, no. I had a job working for the writer Margaret MacIntyre but it fell through. And when Finn offered to help, I didn't even know who he was!"

The king raises an eyebrow and for a moment, I see

flashes of Finn in his face. Except that there's no hint of kindness or playfulness in his expression. "You'll forgive me if I find that hard to believe."

"It's true!"

The king clears his throat. "I don't begrudge you your fun. But it has to end. Now. Finneas is in a delicate position with the family, the press, and the British public. If he doesn't reform his image now, it'll be too late. So if you care for him, even the slightest amount, you'll do the proper thing and leave him alone."

From an outsider's perspective, it would appear as though we're having a conversation about the art on the walls. But in my periphery, I can see Tina, a few feet away, within earshot. I haven't run into her since that day in the barn. She was probably the one to tip off the king about Finn and me. Now she's listening to me get the tongue-lashing she thinks I deserve.

Well, fuck that.

"I'm an adult," I say, finding my voice. "So is your son. We're both capable of making our own decisions. Enjoy the rest of your evening, Your Highness."

With that, I leave as quickly as I can without drawing attention to myself. My face is hot; my heart is racing. I need fresh air. More than that, I need Finn.

I'm so upset, I don't realize that I've gone out the wrong ballroom door and am now in the red hallway with all the creepy statues. I haven't been in this part of the castle since my first day when Finn gave me the tour. My body's on autopilot and it takes me to the place I felt sparks with him. The place I loved most.

When I reach the library, the light is on, the door ajar. I'm about to brazenly push through it when I hear voices.

"Beatrice—"

"I know, Finn. I know. But all I've been able to think about since I arrived is that I made a mistake. We belong together. You just knew it before I did."

My breath catches in my chest. I look through the crack in the door in time to see Beatrice gracefully wrap her arms around Finn's neck and kiss him.

They're kissing.

I back away from the door and squeeze my eyes shut. I feel like I'm going to throw up. My chest hurts from the breaths I won't exhale; tears are streaming down my face. It's happening. It's happening again. Only this time, it isn't some high school boyfriend I would have never stayed with long-term. This time, it's *Finn.*

I run down the hallway before they can hear me cry.

25

I can't breathe in this stupid dress, but I can't seem to unzip it myself. It doesn't matter. I'll go to the Edinburgh Airport wearing it. I just need to get out of here.

My suitcase is open on my bed and I'm stuffing things into it at random. I've never packed this way—I'm always systematic. I don't recognize myself tonight. I don't recognize who I've become.

Who gets a setback with their dream job and settles to work retail because a hot guy tells her to? Who sacrifices writing time to hook up with a fuckboy prince? Everything I've worked toward, everything I've planned, has been dumped for a guy who was playing me. I'm so angry at myself I could scream. I'm so angry at *him* I could run him over with one of his many cars.

"*Stupid, stupid,*" I say out loud, sitting on my bed, a fist to my forehead. I don't want to cry even though the pressure of all these emotions is making my skull pound.

I judged Margaret MacIntyre for blowing up her life for a guy and then immediately did the same thing. Even after what I went through with Dean. I hate myself. I hate myself so much.

There's a knock at my door. I may be an idiot, but I know it's not going to be Finn. He's probably having sex with Beatrice in the library by now. The library that *I* loved. So who's showing up here? Maybe Caro? I can't face her—or anyone else who may have come looking for me. Unfortunately, the knocking continues. There's a chance it could be an emergency. I relent and answer the door.

Tina, in her silver satin gown with matching gloves, her gray-streaked hair pulled into a tight bun, stands still on my doorstep. I flash back to her presence when Finn's father was all but telling me off.

"Did the king send you?" I ask flatly. "You all can relax, I'm leaving this place."

Tina notes my haphazard packing job and pushes past me. I nearly quip, *Come on in*, but I don't have it in me to be sarcastic. I'm too hollow and sad. The tears I've been fighting burst through, silently streaking down my cheeks. Crying in front of Tina is not on my list of activities I wanted or planned to do tonight. Not like it matters. I'm all out of dignity. Besides, after tonight, I'll never see her again. I decide to ignore her presence and start refolding my clothes so they'll fit in my suitcase.

"I was in love with the king," she says, her voice clear.

Proud. I stop folding. "We were young, this was long before he met her majesty the queen. Our paths crossed as the paths of certain families do. You see, my mother was the curator of the royals' art. My father was a driver. Back then, Augus—*his majesty*—was so kind and warm."

"Like Finn," I murmur, despite myself. I see her nod out of the corner of my eye and decide to give her my full attention. I sit on the bed and indicate the nearby chair in the breakfast nook. It's my way of telling her to take a seat. That I'll listen.

"Yes. Kind and warm like Prince Finneas," she agrees. She sits, her posture ramrod straight. "I was certain the attraction was mutual. One day, we were both at a gallery where Mother was introducing the royal family to a new local artist. As they discussed the artist's works, his majesty and I snuck off to a quiet floor. He kissed me in front of a Chagall."

Tina gets lost in the memory I'm suddenly anxious to climb inside and see for myself.

"What happened after that?" I ask.

She holds her head high. "What happened afterwards is of no consequence. I simply came here to tell you that I've been in your shoes. I've fallen for someone who's out of reach, praying that a miracle would occur, that we could 'buck tradition,' so to speak, and be together. I came here to tell you, Hannah, that believing in such fantasies is as preposterous as trying to live in a fairy tale."

Truth be told, as much as I love books and stories, I've never liked fairy tales. Not the original morbid ones, not the sanitized modern ones. I've always preferred my heroines to be ambitious and calculated. To go after what they want instead of letting life happen *to* them.

Before me is a woman who chose a difficult path. I can't wrap my head around it, but I have a newfound respect for her.

"How can you work here? After everything that happened?" I ask Tina. I saw Finn kiss Beatrice and immediately decided to get as far away as quickly as possible. Tina, on the other hand, took a job with the royal family. She's dedicated her life to running her first love's household. From what Finn's said, she basically raised him and his siblings. "Isn't being faced with all of this on a daily basis too painful?"

"I do it," she says, "because it's rewarding. I'm good at it."

"And?" I prompt, knowing there's more. There's got to be.

"And I do it to remind myself that *this* is real life. I refuse to let my mind wander to 'what if.' There is no 'if,' Hannah, only what is. I'd advise you to keep the same perspective." She pauses as her words sink in and swim around within me. When she opens her mouth to speak again, the mask of indifference has slipped. There's pain in her eyes. "Please don't torture yourself about something that can never be."

It's the "please" that catches me. For all of Tina's stoicism, this is a woman who was hurt from love. That time she cornered me in the barn, she wasn't merely trying to protect Finn—she was trying to protect me too.

I should have listened.

I rise off the bed and give her a hug. Reluctantly, she hugs me back.

"Thank you, Tina. You've been very kind tonight. I promise I'll leave, and I won't look back."

As I say it to her, I make myself the same promise.

26

A cab has been called and my bags have been packed. Now all I have to do is leave. It's the hardest part. I'm shaking, I can't think straight. I'm trying hard to regain some sense of control by being pragmatic.

I'll go to the Edinburgh Airport and figure out the soonest I can fly back to Wisconsin.

I'm sure there's a nearby hotel I can stay at if I can't get a flight within the next twelve hours.

Tomorrow I'll write Beverly an email apologizing for my early departure. I'll send a message to Caro.

When I get home, I'll bury myself in writing and getting ready for college.

I can survive this.

I can survive this.

My suitcase bounces and tips on the cobblestones. I have to lift the hem of my dress to stop from stepping on it. My heavy backpack irritates the skin on my shoulder with every slippage. I keep moving despite these small difficulties. I keep moving despite the ache in my chest that's becoming so painful it hurts to breathe.

"Hannah," a faraway voice cries out. I hear running and then a louder "*Hannah!*"

I'm under an old-fashioned streetlamp at the bridge. I should pretend I can't hear him. I should cross it without a word. But that isn't who I am.

"I called a cab," I shout to Finn as he runs toward me. "It'll be here soon. I just have to get past the gate."

His hair is a mess, like he's been running his fingers through it in all directions. His eyes are wild, his face full of the same shock I felt when I saw him kissing Beatrice.

"But why are you going?" he says, out of breath. "What did my father say to you?"

His father? That conversation feels like it happened a million years ago. I right my suitcase so it'll stand on its own, and let my backpack fall onto it. He has no idea what I saw. "You think I'm leaving because of something your dad said?"

"Aren't you?" he asks. The whites of his eyes are bloodshot, threatening tears. I want him to pull me to him, to tell me it's all a mistake.

He takes a step closer. "Why else would you be leaving so suddenly? Ethel told me—"

"Ethel doesn't know why I'm leaving," I point out. The depth of his betrayal—especially knowing what I've gone through with Gigi and Dean—boils up and over. Pointing a finger and glaring with every ounce of humiliated anger I've got, I practically yell, "*You.* You are the reason I'm going, you lying, cheating—"

"Hold on, wait." He looks genuinely surprised. His eyes close and something akin to relief passes over him. "No, Hannah, sweetheart, did you see us in the library? Beatrice thought she wanted to get back together with me and tried to kiss me, but I obviously pulled away and told her my heart was with someone else. I don't want her. I want you. I choose you. I promise nothing happened other than Beatrice making a move I absolutely refuted. You can ask her—we can go ask her together, you'll see—"

His words are jumbled in my mind, and I have to arrange them and rearrange them to see how what he's saying versus what I saw makes sense. The explanation, his promise of having Beatrice verify everything, settles. My shoulders drop. Of course I believe him. The Finn I've grown to know, grown to *love,* wouldn't betray me.

I choose you.

The echo of the words he said to me the night in Stratford, he meant them.

And that's why this is all that much harder. That much more unfair. Because it doesn't change what I'm going to do tonight. What I promised Tina I'd do. The mixed-up emotions in my chest, in my throat and eyes and limbs, all tighten and release, coming out in jagged sobs. I don't want to say goodbye.

"No, darling, don't cry." Finn cradles my cheek in his hand and wipes away a tear with his thumb. The gesture is familiar, comforting, and it's absolutely wrecking me. He smiles sadly at me and says, "It's all right now. It was a mistake. You just saw something out of context. I never want to lie to you. I never want to upset you."

"It isn't just Beatrice," I whisper, trying to catch my breath.

"What did my father say to you at the ball?" He pulls me into his chest and wraps me in the safest embrace. "He can be an icy wanker, I know. Don't worry about him. We can be together. I'll tell my parents to piss off. We can stop sneaking around."

"No, Finn," I push away. I can't succumb to this. Yes, this moment is easy, it's beautiful, but it isn't real. The longer I live in it, the worse this is going to be. I have to cut this off now. "It isn't just Beatrice, and it isn't just your father—it's *all of it.* This isn't possible. Our lives, our goals—nothing aligns. Better to end it now than to fall for you any further."

"But—"

I see my words "fall for you any further" permeate. He takes in their sweetness, their truth, and combines it with the other truth I've just uttered.

We need to end this.

"It's over." The words come out resolute. "Goodbye, Finn."

I walk away under the moonlit sky, sure this separation will kill me. I want to sink into the dusty ground and cry until there are no more tears. Instead, I pass through the gate and find the cab waiting to take me away from Inveresk Castle. Away from Finn.

27

Caro: I can't believe you missed seeing us at Fringe. I kept hoping magic would happen and I'd hear your laugh in the audience.

Hannah: I know. I hate that I wasn't there. According to the reviews, I missed quite the experience!

Caro: DO NOT READ THE REVIEWS. NEVER READ THE REVIEWS.

Hannah: Even if one called you three "unexpected and hilarious"?

Caro: Oh, go on. Literally. Is there more good stuff?

Hannah: Another one said Perimenopausal and Knackered are "insightful absurdists sure to make you belly laugh."

Caro: OMGGGGGGGGGGG

Hannah: You seriously didn't read a single review? What about Duffie and Leah?

Caro: We all swore we wouldn't. That stuff gets in your head. Do you know who did show up to one of our performances though?

Hannah: Ethel told me she and Beverly came to all of them!

Caro: Aye, they did. Love them. Also . . .

Hannah: Yes???

Caro: Prince Finneas came to one too. Brought these dead brilliant friends with him who laughed their erses off. One of them, Callum, is dating my cousin Kent now.

Caro: Hannah? Is it okay that I tell you this? Are YOU okay?

Hannah: Of course I'm okay. I'm excited for you. That was really nice of Finn to show up. And Callum is wonderful.

Caro: Babe, how are you really? All ready for uni?

Hannah: Getting there.

Caro: Okay, I was looking up your school and now I need you to explain to me why it's called Northwestern when it's not in the northwest.

Hannah: It is! It's in the northern part of the US and it's in the Midwest.

Caro: BABE. I looked at a map. The state of Washington is in the northwest. If you split the US down the middle, Illinois is on the east side. Please ask your professors to explain themselves when you get there.

Hannah: I miss you so much, Caro.

Caro: Perfect. Then you'll be keen to come to Scotland next summer for my wedding.

Hannah: WHAT?????? TALK ABOUT BURYING THE LEDE!!! AHHHHH!!! Congratulations!!! I want to hear all about the proposal and the plans next time we talk. Give Duffie a congratulatory hug from me!

Caro: Will do. Love you. Go pack. We'll FaceTime soon.

Hannah: Love you too.

Once again, chatting with Caro has lifted my spirits. I am beyond thrilled for her and Duffie. The road may have been rocky, but they're clearly where they need to be. Still. There's a pinching in my chest. I wasn't expecting her to mention Finn, even though I'm always so tempted to ask her how he is, what he's doing, if he's okay. The image of leaving him the night of the ball never gets easier to recall.

I take a deep breath and look at the Jane Austen quote on my vanity: "I wish, as well as everybody else, to be perfectly happy; but, like everybody else, it must be in my own way."

I'm overjoyed for Caro: for the success she had at the festival, for the way things have worked out with Duffie. That's not the way my story is going to end. Not the one I'm still writing and not the one I'm living. I have to accept that Finn and I are not meant to be.

I finish folding my sweaters and stack them neatly into a bin. I begin painstakingly wrapping souvenirs from past vacations in tissue paper and putting them in a box. Doing so takes me right back to the gift shop at Inveresk. There are a million things that remind me of my time there. And when the pain of missing Finn gets to be too much, I picture Tina in my cottage, telling me the hard truths about her life. I don't want to live with that sorrow every day. I don't want to have to harden myself against the love I feel. And the best way to do that is to cut off all contact with him. All thoughts of him.

I leave the rest of the souvenirs for the end and move on to my books. I can't bring them all with me to Northwestern, so I focus on my comfort reads, my special editions with sprayed edges.

"Tinkerbell," my mom calls from downstairs. "You have a visitor."

"Okay," I call back. I pause, not allowing myself to irrationally hope that it will be Finn. *He's not part of my future; he's part of my past,* I remind myself. I descend the staircase and see Gigi. She's wearing short-shorts and a T-shirt from some volleyball camp. Her hair has grown slightly longer since I last saw her. It's pulled away from her face, giving me full view of her worried expression.

Even though I've been home for weeks, we haven't spoken since that disastrous phone call when I was still in Scotland. We haven't seen each other since I confronted her about Dean.

There was a time when I would've turned around immediately and gone up the stairs without a word. But she looks so tortured, I can't bring myself to leave her. More importantly, I finally feel strong enough to handle this conversation.

Neither one of us is saying anything, so my mom fills in the awkward gap. "So nice to see you, Gigi. Can I get you something to drink? A snack?"

"Do you want to talk in my room?" I suggest, much to my mom's disappointment. I'm sure she's dying to know what's going on between us. Gigi nods and follows me upstairs.

I let Gigi into my room and close the door behind us, knowing my mom will probably hang out in the hallway and eavesdrop. At least we have the illusion of privacy here. We both sit down on the floor and cross our legs out of habit. For some reason, sitting on the floor is where we'd always end up. Not on the desk chair, not on the bed, but on the floor, where we could paint our toenails and scroll through our phones. I remember sleepovers when we'd stay up late trying to flip each other over by leg wrestling. I remember her telling me about her first kiss while sitting on this floor, and me telling her when Dean and I decided to have sex.

The hardest part about Gigi's betrayal was losing the good stuff too.

She clears her throat. "I don't know what to say to make things better because I don't think I *can* make things better. So I'm just going to say the truth."

"Okay."

She flicks her eyes to me. I don't think she was expecting

me to hear her out. She bites her lower lip nervously. "Here's the truth, then. As ugly and deranged as it is. I developed feelings for Dean, which I shouldn't have done, and acted on those feelings. More than once. In the process, I hurt you, which kills me because you're one of the people I care about most in this stupid world."

"You can't help who you love, Gigi," I say, knowing this better than anyone. "But when you acted on it instead of talking to me? That's what I can't get around. The fact that it went on for as long as it did . . ."

"I know." She buries her face in her hands. It becomes clear in this moment that she's going to punish herself and hate herself more than I ever could.

As hurt as I am by her, I don't hate her. She was a good friend to me for a long time. I don't want her to be miserable. There's one thing I can do to help her in this moment, one thing I can do to be a good friend to her, whether she deserves it or not.

And so, right here and now, I choose to let my anger go. I take all the pain of her betrayal and let it slip through my fingers.

It's easier than I thought it would be and makes me feel lighter than I have in months.

"What you and Dean did was epically shitty," I tell her. "It cost you our friendship. We'll never go back to what we were."

"I know," she says.

"But."

"But?" She looks up hopefully.

"But I do miss you," I say, because it's the truth.

"I miss you so much," Gigi says, quiet tears streaming down her face. "And I can't believe we're going off to college not being friends, and on top of all that? We have to be, like, adults now."

I laugh. Gigi's never been the responsible one between us. Obviously.

"You'll survive," I tell her. "If I can handle a summer overseas where I lose my job and my flat in the first forty-eight hours, you can handle living in a dorm a couple of hours from home."

Gigi stops crying. "Wait, what?"

For a split second, it feels like old times. I lean into that feeling and give her the abbreviated version of my summer. I don't mention that the guy I was seeing was royalty. I may be talking to Gigi again, but I still don't trust her the way I used to.

"I don't understand," Gigi says, shaking her head. "If you loved him and he wasn't really with that Beatrice chick and you misunderstood what happened, why did you still leave? Why aren't you talking to him anymore?"

"It was too messy," I say simply.

"Yeah, but . . ." Gigi's eyes look down. She pretends to examine her nails. "Sometimes messy is worth it."

I don't need to hear what she means by that. I don't

want to know if or how she and Dean are in love, despite their ugly beginning. Still, her words sink in. More than I'd like them to.

"I should finish packing," I tell her, standing up. Even without the anger I've been harboring, I only have so much emotional bandwidth for this reunion.

"Yeah, of course." She hastily stands too.

There's an awkward moment where we'd normally hug. I check in with myself, decide I'm ready for that step, and wrap my arms around her.

"Good luck, frosh," I say.

"Good luck to you, fellow frosh," she replies. "I'll only be a couple of hours away if you get lonely at Northwestern."

I nod. I can't commit to that, but that doesn't mean I want to shoot the suggestion down completely. I don't know what the future holds for Gigi and me. I don't know if the mess she and I have made will be worth it. But, right now, I'm willing to keep that door open.

28

I'm lugging suitcases and giant boxes of my belongings down the stairs, wishing I would've taken my phys ed teachers a little more seriously when they talked about the importance of muscle mass. I may have spaghetti arms now, but by the time I set up in my dorm at Northwestern, I'll be jacked.

When I reach the front foyer, I catch a glimpse of my parents seated in the living room.

"No, no, don't get up," I say sarcastically, out of breath. "I've got this."

"Can you come in here, Tinkerbell?" my dad says, ignoring my tone.

Oh, lord. They're finally going to announce their divorce, I think, slightly stressed about fitting everything into my car. I flop onto the couch. I've been home for a month, and in that time, I've filled my days with volunteering at the library and working on my manuscript (I'm closing in on the third act; I just haven't decided how it should end). What I haven't done is spend much time with my parents. Looking at them now, I can see how tired they both are, the worry in their eyes.

"I'm going to be okay, you know," I say preemptively, just in case this isn't a we're-getting-divorced talk and it's actually a please-be-a-responsible-college-student talk.

"We know you will be," my dad says.

"You're going to be more than okay," my mom adds.

It hits me in this moment that, as much as I'm ready to have my independence and get away from the toxic dynamic between the two of them, I'm going to miss my parents. For all their faults—for all the ways they pushed me to grow up faster than I should've, for the ways I was forced into being organized and structured because they didn't have their shit together as people or as a couple—they did their best and they love me.

"What's this about, then?" I ask, since they're both fidgeting, exchanging looks.

There's a pause before my dad speaks. "We weren't there for you when everything happened with Dean and Gigi," he says slowly. "And we—"

"But that's because you didn't tell us about it," my mom interjects.

My breath catches in my chest. I wasn't expecting this. I *knew* my mom would eavesdrop. Since thinking about Gigi and Dean doesn't sting anymore, I'm basically just caught off guard. But then a frustration I've been bottling up about all this explodes out of me.

"It's hard to tell you two about stuff when you won't stop complaining about each other to me," I point out.

"Well—"

Whatever excuse my mom is about to give me, I'm too tired for it. I love her and she needs to hear this.

"You two have a lot of great qualities," I say evenly. "But I have to carry all my baggage *and* yours some days. You both rely on me as your sounding board, I'm the person you vent to. That isn't fair, especially since I am very much in the middle of you two." When neither one of them responds, I add, "Scotland gave me a break from all that and made me realize I don't want to do it anymore. I don't want to be the one in charge of keeping you two together."

My dad swallows hard, and my mom's face goes pink. I've hurt them. It's unpleasant. It also feels necessary.

"I'm not your marriage counselor," I tell them. "I'm your daughter. I love you both and I need you two to figure things out while I'm away this year."

They still aren't speaking, whether it's because they're shocked or ashamed, I don't know. Because I'm not a total monster, I give them each a hug and tell them I love them. Then I go back to the task of hauling all the stuff from my room and the kitchen supplies I'll need to the front door. They stop me at the entryway to the kitchen. My dad takes the box containing a mash-up of random dishes, cutlery, and a couple of small appliances out of my hands. My mom comes in for an awkward hug.

"I'm so sorry, sweetness," she says, giving my back a rub.

My dad wraps his arms around my mom and me and says, "We both are."

I let them hold us all together like that for a beat before I say, "So what are we going to do about this dysfunction?"

My parents exchange a look. I don't know what I'm expecting them to say. That they'll give counseling another try? That they'll divorce? That they'll have an open marriage and I should be expecting larger Thanksgiving gatherings from here on out?

Finally, my dad speaks. "I don't know. I really don't."

Mom takes his hand and gives it a squeeze. Addressing only him, she says, "Maybe it's okay to not know."

I sigh. These two bozos are lovable, despite everything. Maybe it really is okay for them not to know now. "Tell me when you figure it out, will you?"

"You'll be the first to know," my mom says.

A weight I've had on my back for years lifts. I told them a truth, they told me a truth. It's enough for now.

"Let me go get my outdoor shoes and I'll give you a hand taking all this stuff to the car," my dad says.

"So will I," my mom says.

They're clearly feeling guilty. I can't say they don't deserve to.

I lift one of the bigger tubs of clothes, knowing I should probably put it in my car first and pack around it. I manage to push the handle on the front door and pull it open. And then I drop the tub of clothes on my feet because Finn is on my doorstep.

Finn.

Is on.

My doorstep.

"What are you—why are you—when did you—why are you—" Words won't come out, but, embarrassingly, hot tears flow freely. I've missed him more than I've allowed myself to acknowledge. Plus, I just really hurt my toes by dropping the tub on them.

"My American Hannah," he says, his voice soft, sad. "I'm sorry for surprising you like this. Are your feet okay?"

"They're fine," I say, having no idea if they are. I may have ten broken toes and not know it because *Finn is on my doorstep.*

Finn's fidgeting; he's more nervous than I've ever seen him. He clears his throat. "I've recently spoken to Caro, and she said you were heading off to uni. I wanted to catch you before you got there."

"Why?" I ask, still in shock. My body is buzzing, and my mind is blank, and I can't help but think this must surely be a dream.

"Well . . ." He scratches the back of his neck. "Once you get there, you'll be surrounded by beefy footballers and academic charmers."

A small laugh escapes my lips. I'm desperate to reach out, to grab him and hold him and not let him go. But there's nothing about us that makes sense. Nothing's changed in that regard.

"So anyway," he goes on. He clasps his hands together, probably so he'll stop fidgeting. "I've had several chats with members of your fan club, determining whether showing up here was a good idea or the most terrible idea in the history of Great Britain—"

"Good idea. It's a good idea," I interject. That grants me a crooked, albeit still nervous, smile. "Wait, who's in my fan club?"

"I don't mean to inflate your ego, but pretty much everyone you met whilst in Scotland. Bethany, Mhairi, Callum; Caro and Duffie of course; and Ethel and Beverly; and my sister Poppy; and Tina . . . shall I go on?"

"Tina's a fan of mine?" I try to remember her reaction when I hugged her. It wasn't particularly warm.

"She is. In fact, she told me a very interesting story about a chat she had with you mere moments before you fled the castle." He looks down at his feet. When he lifts his face, his eyes are shining with tears. "She felt quite bad about it, actually. She thought she was doing both of us a favor, but after seeing me absolutely shattered and talking to me about my feelings for you, she wanted me to pass along a message."

"Really?"

"I believe her exact wording was 'I was wrong, Hannah, *buck the system.*'" He tilts his head. "This is rather impressive as it is the first time in history that Tina has ever admitted to being wrong about something."

I let the words and all my feelings stretch between us like taffy, waiting for something to snap. He's here. *He's here.* I can only imagine how much trouble he must be in.

"Do your parents know what you're doing right now?" I ask.

"My parents have an idea. Speaking of which, I can see yours are obviously aware I'm here." He looks over my shoulder and waves. "Hello, Hannah's parents. I'd love to meet you properly; I just have to convince your radiant daughter to take me back first."

Without looking back, I step outside and close the door behind me. I want to wrap my arms around him, but I'm too scared. Instead, I sit on the stoop. Finn sits down beside me, his palm up. I can take his hand if I want to. I really want to.

But.

"I can't be a fling for you," I tell him.

"I don't want a fling. Clearly. I mean, I did just fly across the Atlantic."

"Yes, that's an excellent point. I live in the US, and you live in the UK."

"Flying is very affordable for me," he says. "I'm voracious about collecting travel points."

I leave that one because I'm not sure if he's teasing or how finances work for him when he wants to go somewhere or buy things. I move on to the most insurmountable issue.

"You're a prince. You're supposed to be with someone special."

"You *are* someone special," he says softly.

"You know what I mean."

He sighs and takes away his outstretched hand, rubbing both palms against his slacks. "Do you remember the first time you rode Rosie?"

I nod, recalling how incredible it was to face a lifelong fear and experience the thrill, the freedom, of riding. He was patient with me and kind. That was the first day I knew there was so much more to him than staggering good looks and charisma.

"You trusted me enough to face your fear. That was the moment my crush on you turned into something more, something deeper. And I promise—if you place your trust in me again, I won't let you down."

The look in his eyes somehow gives me chills and makes me melt all at the same time. He means every word, I can tell.

I know what I want. I know what I need to do to have it.

"Finn?" I say.

"Hannah?" he replies, worry etched all over his face.

I put my hand out between us, my palm up. I'm wordlessly asking him to take my hand. He doesn't hesitate and soon his warm hand is engulfing mine. He brings it up to his lips to kiss it.

"I have a lot of things I want to tell you." I lean my head on his shoulder. "I want you to know how much I've missed you and how I've thought about you every day, every night, and—"

"Hold on," he says, his voice dipping low. "Let's not skip over the part about you thinking about me every night."

I smile and lift my face to look at him. "But most of all, I want to tell you that I'm in love with you."

He reaches out to brush my hair from my face so that he can press soft kisses to my cheek, my temple, my forehead, my nose, and finally my lips. The kiss is full of desire, of promises. It's sweet and powerful all at once and I can't remember why I ever thought I could live without this person.

When we reluctantly pull apart, he says, "In case that reaction muddled things, I'm very much in love with you too."

"So what do we do about that?" I ask him, internally soaring even though I'm still scared of the unknown.

"We figure it out together."

"Together," I agree.

There, sitting on the porch, hand in hand with the sweetest boy I've ever known, I already know that the messiness to come will be worth it for him, for me. For us.

EPILOGUE

Finn

The Deering Library is every bit as impressive in person as it is in photographs. With the medieval-style windows and arched doorways, the library looks a little like a castle. No wonder it's her favorite. And, of course, it makes perfect sense that this is where I'm waiting for my girlfriend. She is a book lover, after all. Not to mention, quite the writer. I finally wore her down and she let me read the first draft of her manuscript. It's as insightful and clever as she is, though not nearly as sexy.

I cannot wait to get her to my hotel room.

Students are buzzing around me, holding up phones in every direction. Let them take their pictures, their videos. My parents have agreed that the most recent tabloids have been an improvement to my wilder days. Certainly, dating an American is a bit of a scandal, but it's the kind that has most people excited. The ones who aren't? I've never listened to people like that anyway.

I look at my watch, anxious to see her. It's only been a fortnight since we were last together, but any amount of time apart leaves me restless and aching for her. She said her study group would be getting out around now. She's expecting to have to drive to the airport to meet me. Doesn't she know by now how much I love to catch her off guard?

The library doors open and there she is, her blond hair glowing in the springtime sun. She's got on a mint-green sweater with a neck so wide, it slips down, giving me a view of that milky shoulder I'm dying to kiss. I have plenty of time to drink her in, since she doesn't see me at first—she's too busy chatting with her friends. But one of them notices the commotion on campus and pulls on her sleeve with one hand, pointing to me with the other.

Hannah drops her backpack and charges down the stairs, running at full speed to leap into my arms and wrap her legs around my waist. She's the only person on this planet my security detail will allow to attack me like this.

"Hello, my darling," I say into her hair, breathing in her scent, living to have her in my arms again. She's holding me so tightly; I feel whole again.

I let her down and she stands on her tiptoes, an indication she isn't about to wait another second to kiss me. I lean toward her, and we both ignore the squeals from the crowd as our mouths reunite. Hands splayed on her back, I pull her into me. She combs her fingers through my hair and tickles my neck. This is a moment that will be all over social media in a matter of minutes. Quite frankly, it deserves that kind of recognition because it is one hell of a kiss. I give her a little dip before we pull apart, which makes the crowd go wild.

Our foreheads still touching, her blond hair shielding us a little from the rest of the world, she whispers, "Hi."

"Hi," I say, matching her grin. "Your fan club is really growing."

"These people ignore me every other day of the week. I'm pretty sure this is for you."

"Your fan club back in the British Isles is thriving. It's only fair I get some attention in your country."

We've already made plans for her to spend the entire summer with me at Inveresk. We'll go to Caro and Duffie's wedding; we'll try to land-yacht again (this time I'll be the driver); we'll attend the Highland games and go riding and be together for weeks on end. The future has never been so exciting to me. I've never lived this much for the now and for the when.

Hannah takes my hand as we begin to walk across campus to where our car is waiting. It's easier to ignore the bustle surrounding us when I've got her to focus on. But she still isn't accustomed to this kind of scrutiny.

I give her hand a squeeze. "Is this all too much yet? Is it bothering you?"

"Is what bothering me?" She bats her eyelashes coyly

at me. “Our superpower is existing in a bubble within the world. I’m very happy in my bubble.”

“I’m very happy with you,” I say, giving her a little tug so I can kiss the top of her head.

Most of my life may have been chosen for me, but this one choice I’ve made for myself, the choice to be with Hannah, is the most important one.

I’m beyond lucky she chose me too.

ACKNOWLEDGMENTS

I've long admired the talented Erica Sussman's remarkable list, and can't believe I'm finally lucky enough to work with her and the wonderful team at Harper, including Erika West, Andy Ball, Julia Tyler, Jenna Stempel-Lobell, Briana Wood, Danielle McClelland, Meghan Pettit, Michael D'Angelo, and Taylan Salvati. Thank you to everyone at Alloy, especially Viana Siniscalchi, Lanie Davis, and Romy Golan. And extra special thanks to Annette Christie for her tremendous help.